HARD TIMES IN BABYLON

RUSTIN THOMPSON

SISU PRESS/2024

Copyright © 2024 by Rustin Thompson/Sisu Press

All rights reserved.
No part of this book may be reproduced in any form or by any electronic or mechanical means, including information storage and retrieval systems, without written permission from the author, except for the use of brief quotations in a book review.

Cover photo ©Rustin Thompson

INTRODUCTION

August, 2072

Where We Stand: A Letter to My Readers

Dear Readers,

As many of you may recall, the small agency founded in 2019 by my father, Stanley Eden, was banned thirty years later during the Republican Purge. After the purge was contained in 2060, he was unable to re-start the company, due to the skittishness of publishers, the takeover by AI of much of the publishing industry, the astronomical cost of paper, and, sadly, his loss of will. Six years ago, shortly after his death, I began sorting through the back catalogue of the unpublished works that were submitted to him over the decades. I began Where We Stand: A Letter to My Readers to share some of the odds and ends I found, in addition to my observations on current political events.

Recently, I stumbled upon a number of pieces—essays, short stories, memoirs, whole novels—all written during and about the Covid One Pandemic of 2020. To my knowledge, none were ever published. I remember Dad telling me—I was fifteen at the time—that he could not find a publisher interested in any of the material, that no one wanted to read about what they had all just lived through. "Maybe in fifty years, but not now," they told him.

Since fifty years have now passed, and we are well into our second year of Covid Four, with over twenty-three million already dead and at least twenty thousand dying every day, I'm going to share in this column one of the novels I discovered, written by a little-known author, Richard Duvall.

Readers may see a reflection of themselves in these pages, or similarities to our own ongoing crisis, or even clues as to how to cope. In one scene in particular from the book, Duvall imagined an America very much like the one we find ourselves in now: divided into tribes, living in segregated communities, with the reality-based population, essentially virus-free, protected by walls and security cameras, while those outside the walls, consumed by delusion, are dying by the thousands and resorting to cannibalism. Here is the relevant passage, conceived as a daydream by the author:

He closed his eyes, listening to the lake trickle into a stream, and the nearby buzz of a bumble bee, and visualized a future United States where neighborhoods and regions are protected by drawbridges and checkpoints, walls and electrified fences. The people within, vaccinated against the virus . . . would have their own privatized internet and sustainable food supply. Solar arrays on every house and every car, forests to roam through and lakes to splash in. A land of harmony, while outside the walls the president's disciples will live like cannibals on scorched, disease-ridden plains.

These words have proved to be prescient.

Patricia Eden

> In the hour of the wolf,
> just before the dawn,
> Hard times in Babylon.
>
> Eliza Gilkyson, 2000

1

CAUTION

Yellow tape, reams of it, stretched over the sandbox, under the benches, and across the water fountain.

It circled the merry-go-round and slid down the kiddie slide and lay atop the picnic table.

It formed an elastic noose that hung from the zip line and cinched together the two toddler swings in a waxy knot.

Richard stared at the swings. The tape was the same color as his old python cowboy boots, now faded to a pale butterscotch, and it slithered throughout the playground like a freshly shed snakeskin.

Words were printed on the tape, in an eerie rhyme: *Caution Cuidado Caution Cuidado.*

Old-growth Douglas Firs shadowed the playground. A tiny stream burbled down towards the lake. Even on this chilly morning, with rain expected later, the playground would usually be filled with the chatter of toddlers and happy whoops from the kids on the zip line. Parents looking at their phones. Friends talking with friends. Parked strollers with sleeping babies. But now, only two days after the governor closed everything, the playground already had the feel of a long-dead place, evidence of a cataclysm historians would no doubt struggle to describe.

Richard took out his phone, touched the camera icon, and swiped to the video setting. He began rolling on the toddler swings, the deserted playground in deep focus, the timer advancing. Ten, eleven, twelve seconds. Nineteen, twenty. Then, abruptly, he felt something fall inside him. A deep, sharp plunge in his gut, like a bolt driven into the stomach lining, followed by a chemical surge of fear. He stopped recording and lowered his phone. His hands were shaking. A gust of wind rattled the tape.

2

SOMETHING

"I'll be back in an hour or two," Richard said to Beth, who stood in the kitchen waiting for the microwave to reheat her coffee.

"Have fun," she said. "Wait, I didn't mean . . . you know what I meant."

"I know," he said. Beth took her coffee upstairs to write in her journal and Richard closed the back door and cut through their yard into the alley. They were allowed to go for walks or runs or bike rides, but were told to keep these interludes short, and to avoid other people.

Everything looked like a normal Sunday in their neighborhood. There was the man who volunteered to pick up litter out stabbing fast food wrappers and paper cups, the retired teacher throwing a ball for her two enormous dogs, a church shuttle lowering its wheelchair lift, and there was the same plastic tricycle Richard had seen four days ago, still tipped over in a driveway. But these vignettes, usually so routine as to go unnoticed, were now marked in some way. They carried a charge. The pink, green, and blue flower sketched on the sidewalk next to the tricycle seemed to be vibrating, the splinters of chalk in the grass resembling shards from an archeological dig.

Most of the young families were still in their pajamas, the kids watching cartoons on YouTube, the parents reading the *Seattle Times* online, distracted by the texts from relatives and friends scattered around the globe. The immigrant families in the public housing units were . . . well, he assumed they were doing what most large families did. Laying out breakfast. Taking turns in bathrooms. Scheduling the use of the family van. There were many children in those units, and two parents, and often a grandmother and maybe a grandfather, so they must be crowded and would seem even more so now. Richard smelled coriander and ginger coming from one of the apartments, a mother already stirring a pot of goat stew, preparing to feed generations.

He looked over at Abdul's place, to see if he might be outside working on a friend's car. Abdul was the only Muslim in the neighborhood he talked to regularly, short conversations mostly, but more than the brief good mornings he said to the women. Richard always smiled at them, the mothers and grandmothers, and made sure to say hello to their toddlers and was friendly with their teenage sons, a subtle wave or a thumbs up or a nod, hoping to convince himself the abyss between them was only a matter of nuance. Once he considered inviting Abdul and his family over for dinner, but this was before Abdul had knocked on their front door to ask him something and his eyes flashed to the framed movie poster of *Breathless* on their living room wall, the title written in Italian, *Fino all'ultimo respire,* and featuring the actors Jean Seberg and Jean Paul Belmondo in bed together, Seberg in her modest underwear and Belmondo shirtless and smoking a cigarette. An ashen expression of deep disappointment, or was it embarrassment, crossed Abdul's face, as if he'd wandered into a carnal den of premarital sex and tobacco. Richard then knew that it was not nuance but a gulf of cultural dissonance that separated them.

At the very least Richard worked at appearing non-threatening, since he knew that with his gray moustache and goatee—and a troubling paunch—he could easily be mistaken for one of the president's white supremacist supporters, all of whom were right now mourning the fact that their leader's reelection rallies were postponed. Most people in America thought of this as a kind of unexpected gift the pandemic had delivered, like a cancer temporarily in remission.

Richard stopped to plug his ear buds into his iPhone, and clicked to the archived recording of his radio show from a week ago. *You are tuned to KBCS 91.3. A world of music and ideas. I'm your deejay Richard Duvall, and this is Road Songs.* The radio station had suspended live programming indefinitely, so this was the last installment he'd produce for the foreseeable future. If the apocalypse was indeed coming, he wondered if this recording would still exist in ten years, or fifty or a hundred, after ivy strangled the station and choked off the radio towers, after cobwebs claimed the hard drives. He wanted to make sure his show was worth remembering, a vestigial scrap of sound from what some were already calling the Before Times.

He'd been volunteering at the station for twenty-one years, since right after his fortieth birthday. Independent, community radio, with a strong signal and a loyal audience, holding its own against the tide of smart speakers, AI algorithms, streaming sites, and automation. The goal for his show had always been to create landscapes for the listener, two-lane highways and honky-tonks and lost nights of the soul, scenes of hard-luck cinema. He looked forward to selecting the music, setting the narrative mood, taking listeners on a journey through the crossroads of alternative country and folk—although these labels were malleable, and he often inserted deep cuts of rock and pop and blues into his playlists. He'd been careful never to assign Road Songs an importance that would leave him grieving if it was taken away, but now that the pandemic was official, and the station had indeed converted most of its programming to an automated format, he wondered how long before his audience drifted over to Spotify and Pandora, never to come back. His show, maybe live radio itself, would become irrelevant.

The music he played was like a balm, helping to keep his private checklist of worries on the back burner. But now, an invisible pathogen had brought those worries front and center: his withering cash flow, a dwindling interest in exercise, his feelings of uselessness, an inclination to panic over small things, and his advancing age, which made it pretty unlikely he would start any kind of a new career, and which caused the women who gazed his way to avert their eyes, as if they were looking at the Unabomber or an incel. He was most aware that he was living in a state of artistic oblivion, and that this was approaching an advanced stage, the major symptom being an ongoing accrual of diminishing returns.

His latest film was ignored by funders and distributors and sales reps—the gatekeepers of the documentary industry—and another one of his films was now shelved in mid-shoot. His book on low-budget documentary filmmaking, published two years earlier, had sold maybe three hundred copies. He had no idea who was reading it and often wondered why anyone would. The website he'd carefully designed to help sell his book and provide a platform for his documentary reviews, which he proclaimed were written outside the "mainstream echo chamber," was universally ignored, primarily because he did very little to advertise the site and his half-hearted attempts to share his reviews garnered so few page views he stopped sending them to anybody. He had sworn off all forms of social media years earlier as a protest against their contributions to the erosion of democracy, but this left him with practically no avenues for letting people know he existed. Recently he'd heard about sites called Patreon and Substack, which meant that they'd already been around for so long they were now inundated with nobodies like him trying to market their wit and gravitas to an oversaturated audience, an audience trying to market their own wit and gravitas to the same oversaturated audience. To him, it seemed everyone was drowning in this digital sinkhole.

The few short fundraising films he and Beth made for nonprofits had begun to feel desultory, a kind of mute button against the low beat of despair he would hear if he turned up the volume. There were pleasures, sure: His wife, his grown children, hiking in the forests and alpine tundra of the Pacific Northwest mountains, his love of cinema and music, and books about cinema and music, his radio show and the NBA and handcrafted microbrews. But creeping over all of this was a pall of self-pity.

He'd opened his last show with a three-song set of Simon & Garfunkel tunes—a bit of a departure from his usual playlist, but he wanted to hear Waylon Jennings' whiskeyed baritone singing *The Boxer,* followed by Simon himself with *Wednesday Morning 3am*, his doleful tale of an armed robber on the run, and capped by the singer Tracy Grammer's version of *April Come She Will.* The song was in the repertoire of lullabies he had sung for his kids, a tune of young romance, of seasons turning, but now it contained only portent. April would indeed be coming soon, with its swelling, ripe streams, and things were predicted to get worse: an increase in infections, followed by an uptick in deaths. The coming months—*May, she will stay, resting in my arms again*—what would they bring? Empty store shelves? Power outages? Toilet paper vanished from the face of the earth? Their house was well-stocked from a Costco run he'd made in February, but he did feel a vague alarm this morning when he had to replace a roll in their downstairs bathroom. What were the alternatives: Kleenex? Paper towels? Their hands? Perhaps he should make an effort to use fewer sheets next time.

He crossed the street to a pedestrian path that ran between the townhomes. Fifteen years ago, their neighborhood was transformed from a misbegotten patch of rundown public housing into a well-planned little network of streets, sidewalks, pocket playgrounds, and tree-lined parking strips, a checkerboard of subsidized apartments and market-rate real estate. Three-story townhomes for downsizers like him and his wife, starter homes for young families, temporary housing for refugees. It was named New Rainier Vista because, in late fall, after the leaves dropped, a person could catch a peekaboo view of Mt. Rainier from a third-floor window or a south-facing deck.

There was a central park with a playground, a basketball court, and a field wide enough for games of Ultimate Frisbee. Sometimes he would watch white boys play soccer with the girls in head scarves, laughing, out of breath, and he'd think their neighborhood had found the upside of gentrification. Other times, he'd watch the

Muslim teens shoot hoops, skilled in the argot of the urban American playground but not so skilled with a baseline jumper, and he'd wonder if the cultures could ever truly mesh. A few of the dog owners let their animals run free in the park, and a conscientious neighbor had to remind them that Muslims believed dogs were unclean and that these entitled pets prevented kids from enjoying the park, too. But overall, New Rainier Vista was an agreeable place to live, with a high walkability score. Beth had planted flowers near the sidewalk that would catch a neighbor's eye and Richard would wave to them while sipping a fresh-hopped IPA on the front porch. Most of their neighbors waved back, except for the tech bros who avoided eye contact and cloistered in their bare-walled homes, eating meals delivered by GrubHub or Instacart, trading Bitcoin while devising new codes to control the universe.

August, die she must. He shivered at the possibility of the pandemic lasting until then, or even past September, long after the song had ended. *September, I remember....*

He walked north along Martin Luther King, Jr. Way. The street ran from I-5, where it paralleled the light rail line through the Rainier Valley, before veering towards Seattle's Central District and ending near the Arboretum. Richard had read on Wikipedia that there were nearly a thousand streets named for Martin Luther King, Jr. in the country, and a week ago he was waiting for the light to change at one of these, in Savannah, where he had been working on the now-shelved documentary.

The neon of Savannah's restaurants and bars seemed to quaver in the twilight, the early March air polished clean by a two-day rainstorm, washing away a thick humidity. He was generally in an upbeat mood, happy to be employed on a film in which he was simply a hired hand, which meant he didn't have to worry about funding it or selling it or facing the rejection that inevitably followed when trying to get people to watch it. But despite this good mood, several little things were nipping at him like mosquitos.

There'd been a run on Lysol spray throughout the country and he needed some for tomorrow's return flight to Seattle. His phone pointed him towards a CVS in the historic district, where maybe he could find something else, bleach or baby wipes, that would do the trick. He was trying to envision what the scene might look like at the airport. A surface normalcy probably, but with an underlying thrum, a tangible unease in how people stood, gestured, half-ran with roller bags. Gate agents, aware of the advancing havoc, pecking away at keyboards, fending off platinum club members crowding their desks. Parents jockeying with strollers while holding out their phones to display the glow of their boarding passes. The beeping carts full of the elderly and the disabled parting the crowd at full speed, like hurrying beasts.

Continuing down Savannah's MLK, Jr., passing by The Grey, a restaurant retrofitted from the original Greyhound bus station, Richard thought of the roast quail and mint-dusted cocktail he'd enjoyed there a few nights ago with Shelley. That was another mosquito buzzing his ear, not Shelley, but the film she'd hired him to shoot and cut and co-direct with her. The documentary was, at this early stage, a Hydra of possibilities and tangents, too diffuse for him to get a handle on. They'd been in Savannah for almost a week, after a previous week spent on Sapelo Island, one of the Georgia Sea Islands strung off the state's eastern shore. Shelley was investigating her French ancestry, tracking the history of her fifth-generation great-great-something-or-other, a Royalist sympathizer who fled the revolution in the late 1700s and landed on Sapelo, intending to raise cattle, harvest live oak, and build a seaport for future trading ventures. Instead, he tortured his slaves and went bankrupt, gradually and then suddenly.

Shelley had inherited her wealth: Real estate in Asheville. Property in Seattle. Mutual funds and indexed accounts. She'd founded a film-archiving business and ran it as a nonprofit. She had "a sizeable cushion," she'd told him, yet she was nonchalant about her money. It embarrassed her a bit, and one of the motivations for the documentary was to interrogate the folly and entropy of wealth, the ways in which too much easy cash limited life's choices. At fifty, Shelley had never married and was childless. She titled her film *Died Without Issue*, as in "died without any children having issued forth from her womb." A good title. Self-awareness in the tone of old-fashioned obituaries. It was one of the reasons Richard signed on to the film. But they'd had trouble making inroads with the small Black community on Sapelo. No one returned their calls, and they didn't feel comfortable knocking on doors, two white filmmakers and their frivolous movie, looking to collect a soundbite. They were wrestling with the possibility of simply avoiding the history of slavery on the island all together, but that could raise red flags with the documentary industry's moral guard dogs, on the lookout for any hints of colonial carpetbagging. He so longed for the old days, when storytelling, strong images, high-quality audio, and a respect for the people and places you filmed were all you needed to make a documentary. But now the art form—yes, *he* still considered it an art form—was reduced to an exercise in liberal progressive box-ticking.

Shelley had been the music director at the radio station when he first walked into the place more than two decades ago. She assigned him an overnight shift, a program he called Night Train, featuring slow folk ballads and lengthy world-music tracks. Algerian raï by Rachid Taha or Qawwali by Nusrat Fateh Ali Khan. Haunted chants with lyrics written in Igbo. He liked being all alone in the tiny station during the pre-dawn hours, watching the bouncing VU meters, the electric reds and greens like Morse code from distant lands. He began to identify with misfit deejays, indifferent to grooming, content to speak to the unseen world, surrounded by the soft luster of lighted panels and foam-padded walls. His final act on this earth—if it came down to it—would be to lock himself in the on-air studio at midnight, smoke a bowl, set Townes Van Zandt's "Rex's Blues" on repeat, and overdose on Percocet.

He remembered when Shelley was on the air as a deejay, playing folk music, seducing listeners with her breathy enunciations of song titles and artists. *That was Rock, Salt, and Nails, by U. Utah Phillips.* He was especially glad that they'd stayed in touch all these years, since she was paying him a monthly fee, and this steady infusion from her inherited income might be the only cash he and Beth could count on in the coming weeks.

They talked about this on the phone the night before he was to fly back home. Beth was getting more anxious with each NPR update, ever since the news about mysterious deaths in a nursing home in Kirkland, Washington, only a few miles from Seattle, had broken the week before. The state's governor held a press conference in which he said the killer had been identified as a novel coronavirus that had originated in China, and that people should immediately practice something called "social distancing" and perhaps be prepared to hunker down in their homes. A few nights before, in their lodge on Sapelo, a spacious two-bedroom home on stilts bordering a buggy marsh, Richard talked Shelley into watching *Contagion*, Steven Soderbergh's prescient thriller about a lethal virus. In the film's first act, a character with the Centers for Disease Control ticked off the list of public precautions: Frequent hand washing. Self-quarantine. Social distancing.

"I've never heard that term before in my life," Richard said to Shelley. "And now I've heard it twice in two days."

Beth had just come back from their neighborhood grocery store, and was worried to see it so crowded, nearly all of the carts and baskets in use, people moving briskly through the aisles, stocking up on frozen foods.

"The cashier told me she'd never seen so many three-hundred-dollar receipts."

There was another worry, probably nothing, but Richard had first felt it on Sapelo three days ago: A slight but nagging cough. The CDC and the WHO were just beginning to catalogue symptoms of fever, fatigue, and body aches, none of which he had, but he couldn't help but view the behavior around him on a Saturday night in Savannah through a lens of advancing contagion. Densely packed groups of college students inched along the streets like gigantic caterpillars. A wormy mass of heads and mouths and arms hoisted Jell-O shots and drank flagons of beer in open-air bars. A cluster of shitfaced girls sang off-key karaoke into screechy consumer-brand mics, their faces disfigured with streaks of green and aqua, no doubt the local university colors. The day before, he had been sitting in a bar on Lincoln Street, around the corner from their hotel. The place was dark and low-ceilinged, lit with soot-stained lamps and guttering candles, as if the owners were going for some kind of log-cabin atmosphere evoking the bar's name, Abe's on Lincoln. A man sitting nearby asked him where he was from.

"If I told you, you would kill me," Richard joked, pointing out that Seattle was only a few miles from the epicenter of the blooming contagion.

"Ah, well," the man laughed. "I don't know anything about that."

Maybe current events were on a slow rollout in the South, home to millions of the malignancy's most fervent helper cells. Although Savannah itself had not voted in the majority for the president, the city was probably full of tourists from the hinterlands, the ones who believed Muslims were stealing their jobs and progressives were indoctrinating children into sex-slavery rings. But Richard realized these were knee-jerk judgements, since he had no way of really knowing where the tourists were from or who they voted for. Tonight, they all seemed to be enjoying the city's sophisticated diversions, its enchanting parks and squares, its high-end fried chicken and haute okra.

He patted his pocket to make sure he had his squirt bottle of hand sanitizer with him, a habit he and Beth had picked up during their travels in the developing world. That morning over breakfast, he rubbed sanitizer on his palms after touching the menu.

Shelley said, "Maybe you're going a bit overboard?"

She forked up some grits, which seemed to appear as a side dish whether you wanted them or not.

"Might as well practice a little hygiene," he said, pushing away his own plate of grits, which always looked and tasted like some sort of gravel pudding. "We don't really know what the hell's going on."

"Well, yeah, I'm not really tuned in."

"I can't remember where I heard or read this, but they might start cancelling flights."

"Oh, shit."

"Yeah, I'm glad we're leaving tomorrow."

"You have my permission to keep me updated."

Shelley could afford to rebook them, change fees be damned. If the airports closed overnight, they could buy a car and drive the three thousand miles home. Perhaps a comfortable midsize with a trunk large enough for her meat locker of a suitcase. They'd buy road food from Publix and Albertson's, take turns with playlists from their phones, engage in polite negotiations over the interior temperature controls. Would they run into road blocks? Armed militias?

The sign above the CVS twinkled two blocks away. He headed for it, passing something called a Pedal Pub, where a dozen or so people sat around a mobile bar outfitted with beer taps and bottles of liquor, pumping pedals to locomote the trolley through the town's leafy quarters, erupting in whoops every few minutes and then draining shot glasses. They began singing a pop country song, one of those saccharine anthems to tight jeans and tailgates that colluded with the evangelical programs to swallow up nearly all of the available frequencies on regional radio.

The Lysol shelves at the CVS were empty. The hand sanitizer sold out. Maybe people were getting the message about the virus after all, despite what he'd seen on the streets. He found a suitable alternative to Lysol: lens cleaner, a blend of water, isopropyl alcohol, and detergent. He kept a small supply in his camera bag, but not nearly enough to swab down an airline seat. The cashier bagged the five-ounce bottle of cleaner and a king-size package of M&M peanuts, Richard's usual in-flight snack, and a package of cough drops.

The next morning, he packed the lozenges and tissues and M&Ms in his camera bag along with the camera, its shotgun microphone, a memory card, and one fully charged camera battery. This is one of the essential lessons he'd learned as a freelance news cameraman. Always be ready to leap off a plane and start filming, in case your luggage is lost, or something happens in the air or in the airport that is worth shooting. If the plane went into a nose dive, would he have the wherewithal to pull out his camera and capture the panic of the passengers, the hideous groan of the engines, the blizzard of plastic cups, books, and iPads, the final terror on the faces of the flight attendants—the law of averages having run its course—and the moment of impact? Maybe the memory card would be discovered among the smoking wreckage, the footage of the final careening seconds intact, properly exposed and focused, and this would bestow upon him the kind of fame that had eluded him while alive.

But right now he was only worried how the passengers on the flight would react if his cough worsened from a tickle to a raging hack. Two months ago, he'd come back from a three-week trip to Mexico with a painful cough, something so deep and clawing it felt like a rodent was scaling his thorax. He'd been feverish and fatigued and plagued with night sweats, "the sickest I've ever seen you," Beth had said. On the flight home from Mexico City he had a coughing fit so wrenching he had to smother it with his bandanna and the woman in the seat in front of him turned to stare as if he'd sprayed her with anthrax.

By the time he and Shelley arrived at the airport in Atlanta, the tickle was gone. He felt fine. They had a few hours to kill before their flight home, so they took turns going on long walks, the kind of exercise ever more common in America's terminals, where people gird for the whole-body terrors of domestic air travel. But he grew anxious while walking past hundreds of people and through the spaces those hundreds had just walked. Was he waltzing through an aerosoled mist of contagion? Could the airport be a convergence zone of vectors for a pathogen most people hadn't even heard of yet?

The airport's loudspeaker system clicked on and a man's voice was heard above the babbling din, announcing a prayer service starting in an hour in Concourse D. Richard thought this was odd at first, but then he remembered he was in the Bible Belt and the airport probably held church services every Sunday. He imagined how that announcement might change in a few months if events cascaded, if they reached a more, um, *cinematic* level. Perhaps the voice would note the latest arrival of corpses on the tarmac. Travelers would gather at the windows to get a look at the body bags and the National Guard soldiers sheathed in Tyvek, the requisitioned military planes with built-in conveyor belts, the bodies silently shuttled in spaced increments to the end of the belt and then forklifted onto pallets like large boxes of fruit. The voice would then announce the prayer service, this time for family members who'd come to the airport to mourn.

One of the perks of traveling with Shelley, he was excited to realize when they organized this trip, was flying first class. But first class did not mean first on the plane. They had to wait for the disabled and the elderly, for the parents traveling with small children, for the military and the first responders. And then the frequent flyers, those whose plans were tumescent with triple mileage bonus points, the Caligulas of air travel.

Finally, now in his seat, he pulled out the lens cleaner and sprayed the pouches and tray and seatbelt and buckle and wiped them all with his bandanna. Next he went to work on the small dial for the overhead vent. The push-button light switch. The controls for the seat back monitor. The safety brochure and the in-flight magazine, with its back page advertising a vacation in the Balearic Islands, one of those paradises he'd vaguely heard of and could see himself visiting one day. Or he used to be able to see himself visiting, before the internet age turned the delight and lure of travel into a tangle of third-party booking, hidden fees, and prices that lurched higher or lower within minutes and without logic, where one moment of distraction would mean you'd paid a bargain-basement price for a flight from Seattle to Los Angeles that involved a twelve-hour layover in Minneapolis.

The ignominy of airline travel was another one of those small humiliations that could send him into one of his nostalgic funks. This depressed him, since he didn't really care for nostalgia, especially as a place of refuge. He'd always thought there was too much living to be done to wallow in the past. But then the process of living began to gray on him a few years ago, and he found himself knocking around in a kind of no-man's land, where he could not look forward and he dared not look backward and when he looked at the present he wasn't pleased with what he saw.

Passengers took their seats around him. The extra leg and elbow room in leisure class made it easier to pretend that the virus, if it was on the plane, was not after him but instead was heat-seeking the peasants jammed together in the cattle pens of coach. The flight, like all flights since 9/11, was full or, as the flight attendants put it, "completely full," as if there was a discernible difference between the two. Sometimes they would describe a flight as "very full," as if the plane was a fat man eating at a Spaghetti Factory, where merely full suggested he could still manage to find room for the berry crisp, but at the level of very full he'd throw up his hands.

Five hours later they descended to Sea-Tac through a tin-colored sky, at that dispiriting moment when daylight began to char to dusk. There were times when he looked forward to the dark Northwest winter. It gave him permission to stop trying to be productive, to surrender to a movie or a book at four in the afternoon. But now the dark arrived with a vague sense of unease.

Beth was waiting outside. He gathered his baggage and said goodbye to Shelley, hugged his wife, and loaded his camera equipment into their car.

He clicked his seat belt and felt it immediately.

It. Something. Not inside of him but outside. Out there. A kind of static in the air, electromagnetic and unnerving, like the moments before a snowfall, but laced with a hint of menace rather than anticipation. They could both sense it as Beth wheeled out of the airport to I-5 for the twenty-minute drive home.

"I was on the light rail a couple days ago," she said. "There was one person on the train wearing a surgical-type mask. Even though the train was packed no one sat next to him, like we all thought he was already infected. It all felt very creepy."

. . .

That evening, Beth shared with Richard the notes she'd been keeping in her journal while he was in Georgia, written in the kind of shorthand she used when she only wanted to record events and places and ephemeral moments:

March 5:

11 deaths now.

March 7:

Crows are calling a very large meeting. Are they aware of how oddly we humans are currently behaving?

March 8:

Today our governor kinda lowered the boom re frivolous outings. In 6 days, we've gone from a handful of deaths in WA to 29. But if you look at Italy, WOW. All of a sudden, 800+ deaths?

Now, Richard stood on Seattle's MLK waiting for the light rail to clear the intersection. The train cars wouldn't be crowded this early on a Sunday morning, but he wondered if the number of passengers could be a kind of gauge of how quickly the world was turning. The first car, then the next, then another. All deserted. In the fourth car was a single passenger, a man sitting near the window. Richard remembered Beth's description of the packed train and the man with the mask. But instead of a mask this man appeared to be wearing some kind of hood, all but his eyes covered. He raised his head and peered at Richard out the window. Their eyes locked for three or four seconds. There was something odd in the exchange of glances, even chilling, as though neither of them dared to look away. The man seemed not to be made of flesh and blood but was instead a kind of apparition or wraith, an afterimage of the train's very last passenger.

The train trilled and the soft rattle of its wheels dissipated, leaving behind an echo of silence. The light changed to green and Richard walked utterly alone through the intersection.

3

PANIC

Vacant train tracks and empty parking lots. Bits of trash blowing up against the Philly cheesesteak restaurant. The closed signs in the Starbucks window. The abandoned wheelchair next to the fort of blue tarps where the homeless man lived. These were scenes from the sci-fi thriller they were now living in.

Richard watched them in wide-screen, as if through a viewfinder. He always looked at the world this way, composing shots while walking, driving, sitting, marking the four walls of the frame, noting the quality and angle of the light, the play of the shadows, the foreground and background. He'd had this habit since he was a teenager and became obsessed with films, going to see anything and everything that came out. The B-movies, the bland movies, the mediocre and the masterpieces, willing to search for something redeemable in even the most forgettable drive-in dreck. His eyes were a movie camera before he held his first camcorder in college.

Maybe he could construct a montage out of these images. The high-school reader board already announcing the postponement of classes. The Wendy's and the Burger King with orange cones blocking the drive-thru lanes. The locked doors of Lowe's Hardware. Wide shots dense with omens of calamity, long shots haunted with dystopian intent. He could set them to a soundtrack of plangent strings or a Gregorian choir.

He had just started to re-read *The Plague*, and he wondered if it would work to narrate passages written by Camus' enigmatic narrator and lay the audio over the images. Trite? Maybe. Or maybe the resulting film could be bracing in its simplicity. Finally, *finally*, he would be discovered. *This* would be the pass he could flash to the gatekeepers who'd always brushed him off. *This* would be his entrée into the rarified pantheon of celebrated documentary filmmakers, that ever-tightening clique of trust-fund socialites and Netflixed insiders. He'd be accepted into Sundance and invited to Cannes. Critics would swoon. 100 percent on Rotten Tomatoes. The Oscar for Documentary Short. Yes, *this* was a good idea, he thought. *This* might work.

The concept excited him, and he arrived at the playground ready to go to work. He pulled out his phone, changed the video setting to 4K, and set it to super-slow motion, which rendered time to a near standstill, producing images that flowed like a thick syrup. There were the toddler swings bound together. An acute image, loaded with meaning. The end of play. Throttled dreams. Parents in a knot of frustration. He remembered the chore of filling the daytime hours when his own kids were little. Even on good days, when they were engaged and happy, it could be a challenge. Now, without the distractions of outings and playdates and preschool, this task would be Promethean.

He framed the shot and began rolling, briefly mesmerized by the metaphorical weight of the image, the slight sway of the swings in the breeze, imagining the quotes from Camus, the immense sadness of it all, the . . . the . . . and then: an acidic burst in his gut, a clutch of panic, as though he were in a roller coaster descending through a hole in the earth. It was a type of seizure. Involuntary and abstract. A thought flashed through his mind. He didn't know what to make of it at first. But then a chill came over him, and he could feel a presence. He reached out a hand to touch it, but it was invisible, out of the frame.

He lowered his camera.

The bottom immediately dropped out of his enthusiasm. The idea of making a film from these pictures and using prose from Camus in voice-over was stupid, *so* stupid, *embarrassingly* stupid. The utter banality of it. *Everyone* will be doing this. *Everyone* with a smartphone throughout *the entire world*—which was everyone—will be documenting the symbolic *grandeur* of the emptied world, the *tragic beauty* of it all. The images will arrive as already tiresome. Flipbooks of visual clichés. The yellow tape rattling in the wind . . . *oh God, what shit.*

He had nothing left to give. Not a single fresh idea or concept. All the images of the world were used up, recycled, used again. The impoverishment of his imagination was complete. Trembling, he tucked his phone away and walked down to Lake Washington.

Truth be told he'd been experiencing a kind of malaise for months now. Not constant, not debilitating, but it was there, off-screen, an unwanted voice whispering now and then in his ear. *Suicide, why not? Give it a try.* Perhaps what he experienced a moment ago was that voice, speaking up, a little louder than before. *Forget it,* he told himself. *Nothing to worry about.* He figured it was a good bet that everybody was going through something similar right now. Perhaps it was only theoretical, this thought of . . . not actual suicide . . . but an academic consideration of the act. To be studied, broken into its component parts, until it was rendered sterile and harmless.

He tried to shake the feeling off as he continued along the lake path.

Spring was holding its breath. Buds remained closed. A heron stood watch at the end of a dock. A cold breeze skittered the surface of the water. There were a few runners, others walking. He was careful to swerve around them, turning his head to avoid breathing their exhalation.

The first hour of Road Songs ended with "Something About What Happens When We Talk" by Lucinda Williams. She sang about the intimacy of the human voice, the long-distance phone calls made from hotel rooms and the front seats of cars, lovers separated by high plains and city blocks. It would not entirely be an awful thing if this pandemic resulted in people using their phones to actually speak to each other, to *reach out and touch someone*, like the old television commercial suggested. It seemed like centuries had passed since the last rotary phone was decommissioned. He wondered if long emails would come back in vogue. Maybe even letter writing.

For years he'd collected the letters of a close friend, Anthony, who knew a thing or two about periodic depression, what he called his "dark stretches." In his letters, Anthony composed ornamental riffs on everything from Magritte to Bukowski to The Flaming Groovies, ending with a punch line about a bad romance or his own artistic failures. Richard stored the letters in an envelope, thinking perhaps one day he'd turn them into a book. But then email was invented, and the letters stopped coming. Anthony's long missives shortened, the emails reduced to a sentence or two. Now he used voice text while driving, his messages arriving in a gnarled syntax, the wrong words standing in for the right words. *Toffee* instead of *coffee*. *Bibles* instead of *bubbles*. Anthony's moods had finally evened out with the help of lithium and his buoyant daughter, the enduring reward of his second failed marriage, and Richard figured his own mood dips were small potatoes compared to his friend's struggles, so he never brought them up.

More phone calls. More literate and thoughtful emails. More stay-at-home dads. There was a story that morning about a man who, after homeschooling his kids for three days, declared that teachers should be paid a CEO's salary.

Several articles were already coming out about the rapid swing to online living, with everyone discovering Zoom, an app which up until now had mostly been used for business conference calls. He and Beth had been forced to use the app last week for a work meeting. It dissected groups of people into individualized blocks, like an ersatz game of Hollywood Squares, promising live cocktail parties and college reunions and remote learning. It seemed that everyone was quickly adapting to this and other scenarios, life lived at the mercy of bandwidth and high-capacity routers, where actual human contact is rendered nonessential. There was some hand-wringing for those who lived in the Wi-Fi-free wastelands of rural South Dakota and New Delhi slums, but these folks could easily be ignored, cast aside like flip phones and VHS tapes.

The aesthetics of Zoom were what rankled him the most: the clickable screen options that bore a diabolical resemblance to convenience-store surveillance monitors; the glitchy audio that ruined crosstalk and destroyed comic timing; the soap-dish visuals—a kind of digital pointillism—that would probably become accepted as a new and radically cheaper way to deliver content. His skills as a cinematographer would soon be considered arcane. He'd become a longshoreman of images no one wanted anymore.

He stopped to use the bathroom near the soccer field, the grass an infertile green, cleared of children, as if some rapture had hoisted them to the heavens. The dank atmosphere of the men's room—the clammy walls, the smell of urine, the weak sodium-vapor light attached to the ceiling—made him think of prisons and the mayhem a contagion could wreak among the incarcerated. He'd once spent a night in jail for drunk driving, when he was twenty years old, after having been behind the wheel of his Ford Comet at two in the morning, swerving down a two-lane road, barbed-wire fences streaking past his periphery, drinking bottle after bottle of Hamms and throwing the empties out the window just to hear the glass shatter on the pavement. He'd blacked out while driving, apparently still able to slalom the Comet around the roadkill and between the drainage ditches, before passing out in a Safeway parking lot, a cop's flashlight searing into his eyes. Fingerprinted and thrown in a communal cell, a large room with bunk beds, he was surrounded by at least twenty other prisoners, like extras from *Cool Hand Luke*, discussing bail amounts and plea bargains. He slept fitfully with his contact lenses in, laying on his back, urgently alert to any murmurs of inmates plotting his gang rape. The next morning, he was cuffed to a long chain in a line with his fellow jailbirds and led into a courtroom. He was surprised—and relieved—to see his mother among the spectators but, at the same time, embarrassed and ashamed. She paid the one-hundred-dollar fine and took him to breakfast at the Royal Fork. Free at last!

A puny, pathetic experience, but it had given him a sharp sense of what lockup could look and feel like, if it were to stretch for days, weeks, years.

He'd also filmed inside prisons. Maximum-security alamos in the vast ranchland scrub. Medium-security campuses on the edges of suburbs. Walla Walla and McNeil Island, the correctional centers in Shelton and Purdy, the sexual offenders' unit in Monroe. These places seemed to exist outside of time, with their heavy iron gates and slamming dead bolts, the coarse rustle of baggy orange jumpsuits and shuffling slippers, a TV tuned to a wildlife show suspended from a corner in the common room.

The daughter of a childhood friend of his had been in jail a few weeks before the virus hit. Lina was twenty-five, a heroin addict. She usually drifted in and out of her dad's home in Tacoma, not far from where Richard grew up. She navigated a netherworld of petty theft, needles, couch surfing, arrest warrants, missed court dates. Sometimes she'd get clean, work odd jobs, then drop out again. Richard wondered if she crashed with other junkies in one of the moldy ramblers dotting the white-trash neighborhoods he and his friend had hung out in, with their warrens of ratty bedrooms, their stained kitchen linoleum, and the peeling countertops. Back then, he would sit on shag carpets, listen to Led Zeppelin on a Magnavox, guzzle Heidelberg and smoke hash. These were the houses where the dope dealers had lived. Was Lina in one of them now, looking at current events through a corroded junkie fog and deciding that this was as good a time as any to clock out, to say fuck it, the world just got even more shitty?

This is how his brain was clicking, from the mundane to the grim, the trivial to the unbearable, from the nonsense of video conferencing technology to the dire astonishments of the dopesick. His own little bout of—what should he call it, ennui?—seemed inadequate, not worth his time, and he vowed to buck up.

A hundred yards west of the soccer-field bathroom, he stopped at the edge of Columbia City, across the street from their local library, normally open for a few hours on Sunday afternoons. This was one of the closures that didn't make sense to him. Libraries provided a service as essential as food, coffee, alcohol, ibuprofen, and cannabis —all items still readily attainable. Why was a book not as necessary as a take-out burger or fifteen grams of sativa? He enjoyed hopping on his bike in the summer and pedaling over to pick up his holds. Last year, he'd spent a few mornings in the sun reading a memoir by Michael Nesmith, the Renaissance man of The Monkees, who, as it turned out, was an heir to the fortune his mother made as the inventor of Liquid Paper. This led Richard to contemplate the end of typewriters, and to wonder who won the war, Liquid Paper or Wite-Out. Could he ever justify reading something so frivolous again?

The wide bank of windows of their sprawling co-op grocery store, specializing in the organic, the cage-free, and the shade-grown, displayed what looked to him to be the normal bustle of a late Sunday morning. The frenzied buying Beth witnessed there had subsided. The meat cases looked to be well-stocked with chicken breasts and grass-fed steaks, the lamb patties a tempting pink. But then his cameraman's eye focused on the baggers wiping down the cart handles. The cashiers spraying disinfectant on the price scanners. Shoppers standing six feet apart while waiting in line.

That morning the news had claimed that "supply chains are holding," but this was not exactly comforting. A chain is made up of links. If one link breaks, then the chain is immediately useless. Pandemonium might ensue. What would that look like? Checkpoints and armed encampments? Random killings? Families gassing themselves in garages? Dogs loosed and forming feral packs? Certainly, the foundation of civilization doesn't depend on a mere chain. Or does it? After all, this isn't Vladivostok before Glasnost, people searching the inner reaches of vegetable bins for the last parsnip.

The five blocks of the business strip were lined with Mexican, Asian, Caribbean, and Italian restaurants; nail salons and hair salons; shops that sold wine, flowers, fashion eyewear, toys, insurance, bikes, espresso, recycled clothing for fashionably graying women, bathroom sinks and toilets, overpriced vintage furniture, car repair manuals, and envelopes; storefronts hawking insurance and investments; two bars, a movie theater, a nightclub, and a members-only establishment for the neighborhood's long-standing Black population. All were closed, except for the bakery. Richard wanted to buy something, a muffin or a savory biscuit, anything that might help them stay in business.

The bakery's tables and chairs had been removed and white lines were taped at six-foot intervals on the floor, as if the owners were following instructions written in some kind of pandemic coping manual. He was impressed by the marks on the floor, as he'd been by the yellow caution tape at the playground and the quickly agreed-upon pact to clear an area between yourself and another person while passing on the sidewalk. Everyone may have been operating in a daze, unsure of the arc of their next hour, but they were holding onto the promise that all of this was temporary and Earth would soon return to its normal rotation. He needed to hold onto that promise, too. He needed to believe that his malaise was survivable, that the convulsive fright in the park was an isolated, one-time thing.

He ordered two tortas from the man behind the counter, who had the look of many of the city's young males, enslaved to the gig economy: Beanie, beard, tattoos, his body sculpted by Crossfit—the latest fad to capitalize on humans' subservience to their vanity—and dressed in an artfully faded T-shirt bearing the name of the defunct but rediscovered indie band Dead Moon. The man had last worked at the alehouse across the street, the first business on the strip to close.

Richard and Beth thought of the alehouse as an extension of their home and business. That's where they talked about their future, their travel plans; where they bitched about clients and commiserated over the state of the country; where they took each of their children for their first legal beer. The tuna melt hadn't changed in twenty years and the same wall prints of English pubs hung above the same tables, but the bathrooms were now gender-neutral. He liked using the one that had been the women's room. He wanted to believe it offered vital clues to the feminine mystique, a lingering scent or a secret message scratched on the wall next to the toilet paper dispenser. A week ago, he'd said to Beth that if the alehouse went under, he'd be devastated. It closed the next day. Is *this* what triggered his suicidal lurch, he wondered, the decathetered kegs of craft beer at his favorite bar?

On the way home he crossed near the light rail station as another train, passenger-less, skimmed down the tracks. A man was out walking with his little daughter. He carried a two-by-four and a large piece of orange chalk. At every corner he was laying the board on the sidewalk, running the chalk along it to make a straight line. He knelt and wrote something on both sides of the line, and then moved on with the board and his daughter to the next crosswalk, where he knelt and drew another line, and wrote again with the chalk. Richard let them pass and then looked at what the man had written, in orange capital letters: SIX FEET.

Six feet, the accepted depth at which a body should be buried (instituted in London during a plague in 1665, Richard later learned), where it can begin to decay undisturbed, far enough underground to prevent animals from digging up a virus-riddled corpse and spreading the contagion. Six feet was also the distance at which a pathogen's energy flagged and it crashed harmlessly to the ground. At least this is what they were all being told.

4

PREPARE

A week had passed since his episode at the park. He'd stuffed his anxiety away, somewhere, like a snail hiding in secluded darkness until it needs to feed again.

An extra copy of the Sunday *Seattle Times* was folded and left on the front porch. A note was attached, from Bob, the delivery man. Beth had left a twenty-dollar tip for him the day before, so he'd given them an additional paper today as a thank you. She was always doing things like that, leaving extra cash and cookies for Bob on Christmas, lending gardening shears or folding chairs to their neighbors, tutoring girls and boys at the New Rainier Vista Learning Center, volunteering at the face-painting booth during the community potlucks. Her generosity was baked into her Nordic heritage. If there was anything Richard had learned from their nearly thirty-three years of marriage it was the undeniable fact that his wife practiced altruism way more often than he seemed capable of doing. As a small gesture, however, he gave the extra paper to the married couple next door. They had two young sons. He figured the boys would discover the tactile joy of old-school newsprint. They'd caress the comics with their fingers and gaze at the saturated colors in wonder, as though they'd stumbled upon cave paintings from the Paleolithic.

The note:

Saw the envelope at the front door yesterday and I want to say "Thank you" for the thought for me to have $20.00 in these uncertain times. Never saw this idea before in my 44 years distributing newspapers part time. I am so happy for what you did. At my age (71 years) I am very cautious and trying to find ways not to be in a cluster (other than church). It is working out fine at the moment. Further, I think it is <u>very important</u> to exercise your lungs. There are many ways to do that i.e. swimming, long walks, strenuous labor tasks and etc. All the previous deaths have been because of lung failure. So to deliver newspapers for 3 hours each morning keeps my lungs in good shape, not to mention blood circulation. Again, social distancing is fine and O.K. but remember your internal organs come first.

The odd locutions were touching: *strenuous labor tasks and etc., not to mention blood circulation.* As was its corner-drugstore advice: *social distancing is fine and O.K. but remember your internal organs come first.* And the revealing personal details: *never saw this idea before in my 44 years distributing newspapers part time, at my age (71 years) I am very cautious.* Had Bob been delivering newspapers since he was twenty-seven years old? Surely, Richard thought, as he ground the coffee beans, imagining with each whirr of the blades that he was eviscerating the entire Republican Senate, the government will take care of this man when the going gets tough.

Richard was trying to make good on his resolve in this election year to not wake up every single morning curdled with fury, but he also knew that Bob the Newspaper Man and millions of others would be the least important items on this administration's to-do list.

Later that morning, they talked to their son Zach, who'd contracted the virus a week earlier. At least it sounded like he'd caught the virus. There was no way to know. The tests that had been developed to detect the contagion were in short supply and, apparently, faulty, despite the president's promises that "anybody who wants a test can get a test." After two days Zach began to feel better, but then his fever shot up, his breathing grew difficult, his fatigue returned, he experienced night sweats and a loss of smell. There was a word for this: anosmia. Richard added it to the growing library of unsettling nouns taking up shelf space in his brain: Lockdown. Ventilator. Triage. Coffin. Anosmia. Lack of smell meant inability to taste. How would Zach cope without the two senses vital to eating? Would he be shriveled down to bone, sucking liquid nutrients from a tube?

This was another thing Richard needed to worry about: his hypochondria, which had occupied him for days on end when he was a kid. He'd stay up late to watch the medical dramas on TV, each of them featuring a different weekly ailment—Lou Gehrig's Disease, cholera, dwarfism—and then he'd go to school the next day convinced he had a terminal illness or a disfiguring pox, with only months left before something would have to be amputated or he'd be consigned to an iron lung. Nowadays he could dispel most health concerns with a quick online search, although with every headache his first thought was still always: brain tumor.

Zach's loss of smell was most likely temporary. He probably got infected while scooping ice cream at the local shop for five-year-olds with runny noses, or maybe at his other job as a Tuesday-night trivia host in a crowded sports bar. Zach worked these jobs, and others, while trying to complete the editing on his first film, his directorial debut, a low-budget indie. He was in quarantine now, his attention span sapped. He could barely focus on reading or even watching a movie, let alone editing his film. Did it matter? The entire movie industry was on pause. Festivals cancelled. Cinemas closed. Studios already shifting to premiering their backlog of movies on the streaming sites. Maybe this was another gift of the pandemic, an end to all those bloated superhero movies that claimed every inch of screen space in the multiplex. Zach's film, an experimental horror thriller he made for around $60,000 (paid for with help from Shelley and a crowdfunding campaign), would maybe be picked up by a studio looking to purchase cheaper, ready-made entertainment for the sheltering-in-place.

Richard and Beth's filmmaking business was also on hold. Their documentary profiles for nonprofits, which they made at bargain-basement prices of less than $10,000 each, usually screened at fundraising luncheons, where hundreds of people crammed into hotel ballrooms, clanking their silverware while the video ran, waiting for the executive director to beg them for their money. These events played out as a kind of capitalist farce, where a nonprofit had to pluck the heartstrings of the wealthy in order to not only pay for their programs but also to pay their staff. He wondered if the rich patrons who financed these missions would now hold onto their fortunes, just in case they needed to buy their way into the virus-free zones of the coming dystopia.

A film Richard had been making as a side project—a cinematic essay about memory, runaway technology, and the climate crisis, or so he described it on his website—was now in the fine-cut stage. He called it *Slow Revolution,* and it consisted of images he'd taken from around the globe in his more than thirty-five years of picture-making. A quilt of moods, ruminations, and long takes, narrated by a fictional character, a woman with a British accent, which he'd figured would lend the movie a whiff of international cachet. He'd sent it to a competitive market held every year in New York, where the gatekeepers called the film "impressive" and a "magnum opus" with "great potential," except that their admiration didn't stop them from rejecting his film without explanation.

Making a living as an artist had become impossible. The rewards were scant and the audiences almost nonexistent. Beth had published one book about her mother's descent into Alzheimer's and had finished her second, a memoir about her lifelong dialogue with faith and doubt. She kept searching for a publisher while writing essays and teaching classes. Her welcoming smile and encouraging tone made her accessible to students, and now, teaching on Zoom, she brought a new intimacy to her classes. But the pay was nominal, and the older they got the more they struggled against a riptide that carried them further away from ever making money or being recognized for their craft. He griped about the shallow prerogatives of the market. There always seemed to be enough cash to design an app or another emoji, but not to support an artist painting a new Guernica or writing the next "Me and Bobby McGee."

Their daughter, Chloe, was in the middle of completing a master's degree in environmental science with an emphasis on writing. She had an eye and ear for observing the intricate connections of the natural world to human emotions, and had published essays and book reviews. In the summer she was a crew leader for the U.S. Forest Service, clearing and building trails. She hauled a Pulaski through dense evergreen forests and down steep drainages. She cut fallen cedars, constructed stairways from stones, shaped berms out of dirt and rock. In her father's eyes, her job was heroic, tending to the earth as though laying hands on the elderly. For now, she was still promised her summer job. For now, the wilderness was still open.

Richard had always told his children they were learning an important skill in today's America: how to live on very little money. They needed to remain childless, keep a low overhead, shop vintage, skip the luxury cocktails. Sometimes, he felt guilty that he hadn't urged his children to seek out more lucrative and stable careers. Insurance or dentistry, coding or software design, or perhaps something in the exciting new field of wearable technology.

They were living a fingertip existence. No one wanted to think too much about the cliff edge they were hanging on to or how far the fall would take them.

In his darkest moments, Richard believed this was it.

IT.

The end of everything.

The virus was simply too smart, too smart for everyone, for the highly educated epidemiologists and the over-degreed doctors, for the politicians and the pundits, for the rich and the poor, for the fortune tellers and the shamans. He wondered if the pandemic might be the *deus ex machina* that would finally reveal the sour Kabuki of the nation, the ways in which citizens pantomimed living, scraping by in an economy built on the flimsy promises of gig work, side hustles, and minimum-wage jobs, while living under the sway of a corrupt and fraudulent loudmouth who had become president with less than 25 percent of the population having voted for him.

At the root of Richard's anxieties was money, the lack of it, and what that lack said about his relevancy as a man, a husband, a father. He worried that Shelley might get a phone call from her accountant telling her that the income from her inherited real estate was circling the drain, that her renters had stopped paying, that the now-deserted movie theater in the colonial brownstone she owned in Asheville was under water, that her exposure was critical and she needed to examine all frivolous expenses. Perhaps it was time, her accountant would say, while scrolling through Shelley's investment portfolio, to shelve her personal documentary, and stop payment on all checks. The contract she'd signed would turn out to not be worth the digital paper it was written on. Richard and Beth would become penniless and, like the nonprofits they worked for, they would have to beg the rich—Beth's father or her fantastically wealthy uncle—for money to live on. He was worried that one day he would become the thing he'd always feared: a loser.

Beth's journal:
April 1:
Grim projections. Really scary. Must ponder how Richard and I can help, besides watching and waiting.
April 2:
Numbers first—946,234 cases worldwide; 47,858 dead. U.S.—214,461 cases; 4,841 dead. New York—83,889 cases; 1,941 dead. I wonder when I will stop doing this. Maybe I could slow down?

Was it too soon to prepare for apocalyptic scenarios, like a dawn escape into the mountains after bedlam engulfed the cities? Or should they stay put and retrofit their house into a fortress to repel the diseased and the desperate? If he offed himself now, that would certainly end his own anxieties, but what about his family's?

To quell the chatter in his brain, he conducted an inventory of their camping supplies: Counted the canisters of compressed fuel.

Organized their water bottles. Double-checked their supply of AA and AAA batteries. Located his headlamp and water filter. Spent $200 online buying warm socks, rain pants, and freeze-dried food from REI.

Then he made a shopping list for the Shangri-La of white people's comfort food, Trader Joe's.

The nearest branch was in West Seattle, across the bridge spanning the railroad tracks and cargo loading docks south of downtown, which opened up to a view of the city skyline and, on a clear day, the Olympic Mountains surging out of the peninsula to the west. The Olympics were a potential redoubt, veined with rivers draining down the craggy throats of ancient ranges, serried forests of evergreen and moss and fern so forbidding even a virus might lose its way.

The headlines blared from NPR as he drove. It seemed that the media had stopped referring to the pathogen as the *novel* coronavirus, perhaps because it had only been novel or new when it was a faraway thing, growing in a wet market in a cramped Asian metropolis—a city of eleven million no one had ever heard of—some gob of milky sputum from a pig's gut, by way of a bat, in a market sloughed with blood, feces, urine, spittle, and hocked snot. Maybe the world had come around to accepting the presence of the virus, but not to the pathologies of the disease it caused: Grating cough. Body-slamming fatigue. Battering headaches. Shortness of breath. Anosmia. Spiraling oxygen levels. Brain fog. Full-body collapse. Once a person was admitted to the hospital, they faced a grueling fight to stay alive. Death followed infection within two to four weeks. The name of the disease, Covid-19, sounded like something from sci-fi, a newly discovered moon on the far side of the sun. Yes, the virus had shifted, from novel to nonfiction to the fantastic.

The national news continued with a troubling report that millions of people in America had begun to believe the rumor that the virus was a hoax invented by Democrats for no other reason than to make the president look bad. Yet the president had also claimed in a press conference that the infection rate from this hoax—this thing that didn't exist—would soon be down to zero and the virus would simply disappear. Richard had made a pledge in the last year to stop listening to any broadcast that included the president speaking, since the sound bites made him want to shatter glass with his fists or tear out upholstery with his teeth. But now the president's voice was inescapable, his grating yawp always at game-show-host decibels.

There was a sound bite from Washington's governor saying that he was closing campgrounds and forests and hiking trails, meaning, officially, that the wilderness was now off-limits. The socks and the rain pants and the dehydrated lasagnas would never get used.

A line ran from the parking lot to the front door of Trader Joe's, a sight Richard had never seen at a grocery store in America, where consumers usually breezed in like they were walking into their own kitchens. People were spaced six feet apart, some checking their phones, others simply standing, looking straight ahead, trying to adjust to the new reality. Richard took this time to envision his expedition through the store. Gauge probabilities of contact. Spot bottlenecks in the aisles. Take alternate routes if necessary. Do not browse. Grab the first item touched. Keep moving. Head down. Eyes up. In and out quick, that's the key.

Was it okay to buy the Before Times comfort foods? The dark chocolate-covered almonds and peanut butter cups, the salt-and-pepper potato chips, the basil plant for homemade pesto, the bargain-priced red blends? Or should they be training their palates to appreciate beans and rice, Ritz crackers, boxed cereals and cans of high-sodium chicken noodle soup? Would they need to begin rationing, like Britain during the Blitz?

Once inside, he asked a cashier if they had a quota on wine. "Go for it," she said.

Two men blocked the aisle containing the pine nuts Richard wanted for their pesto. He held his breath, turned his body sideways, and skipped between them. He felt ridiculous, like a second-story man squeezing through an unlocked sliding door, intent on rifling through drawers. How long would it take, after things returned to some semblance of normal, for performance art to emerge inspired by the pandemic? A *pas de duex* perhaps, with dancers jousting in six-foot-wide parabolas on a blank stage. Richard had been attending a Sunday morning free-form dance group before the pandemic struck. Ecstatic Dance, it was called. Fifty people in a basement studio swirling and crouching and leaping to world music. The attendees were somewhere between twenty and sixty years old, a few with gray ponytails, a couple of chunky guys wearing rainbow headbands, thin older women in linen yoga pants. The curated playlist started with slow trances, surged in rhythm, and then erupted in galloping beats, the room becoming a whirling hive. The dark, low-ceilinged space was perfect for the anonymity he desired, retreating to a corner and intoxicating himself in the music. They used to do this at music festivals, he and Beth, dance to Afrobeat and salsa and cumbia, and then 9/11 happened, and musicians from other countries found it harder to get visas and festivals tightened their belts. Ecstatic dance was a way to reconnect with that part of his history, and he hoped it would help him lose a little weight, but now he shuddered when he remembered the scene: airless, cramped, sweaty, spitting. A perfect Covid-19 baking dish. The woman who thought up the whole idea—"my dream come true," she once told him—was no doubt devastated that her dream had probably been a super-spreader site before anyone even knew what that was.

Super-spreader. There's another word to click and drag to his mental folder.

He swiped his card and bagged the groceries into totes. Yogurt. Kefir. Potato chips. Chocolate. Jam. Wine.

On his way home he stopped at Lowe's for hand soap, Comet cleanser, and Duraflame logs for the small, chimney-shaped metal fireplace in their backyard. The store was large enough to house football games and rock concerts. One could imagine the president braying that the virus was no match for the country's chains of big-box stores. That the sheer enormity of the human need for vinyl windows, storage bins, and light bulbs could never be brought low by an invisible bug. The president and his crash test dummy, the vice president, had already spent many minutes of an earlier briefing extolling the importance of the cruise ship industry. Those gargantuan petri dishes, conducting experiments in tedium and viral load, with their heaving lunch buffets and windowless rooms, "must be saved at all costs," they proclaimed, as if cruise ships symbolized the *ne plus ultra* of the American economy. Never mind that these seaborne gas guzzlers were registered in foreign countries to avoid paying U.S. taxes.

On his way in, Richard walked past the demolition derby of shopping carts and the closed bratwurst-and-a-coke food truck. He saw a man tying lumber to his pickup. Another loading paint cans into his CRV. A woman pushing a cart loaded with geraniums. These vignettes buoyed his spirits. Maybe fathers were finally going to build that backyard treehouse they'd promised. Maybe couples were repainting their bedrooms, thinking of having more sex. He didn't want to dwell on the negative side of isolation: Domestic violence. Alcoholism. Excessive screen time. Siblings at each other's throats. An uptick in suicides. Could this happen? He read somewhere once that in times of crisis the rate of suicides actually declined as people pulled together, trading morbid self-obsession for contributions to the collective goodwill. Maybe the survivors of this pandemic will realize the dawn of a new era. A fresh sense of multicultural joy. Citizens exchanging rugged individualism for communal hugs. An embrace of universal health care and paid parental leave. Free college, high-speed transit, true majority rule, the end of Fox News, solar-powered everything. Okay, so maybe not *everything*. Maybe not victory gardens and a return to the barter system—the trading of farm-fresh eggs for website design—but possibly something along the lines of, you know, Finland.

This utopia seemed unlikely. There were already tweets and memes and Facebook posts ricocheting around cyberspace proclaiming the pandemic a Deep State plot hatched by Bill Gates, Barack Obama, and Anthony Fauci to use 5G networks to spread the virus (no one bothered to explain how this was even possible) in order to turn the world into a socialist utopia where nobody worked, everything was free, and Antifa ran the IRS. Somehow, Greta Thunberg was involved.

. . .

After a speedy and efficient turn through the store, followed by a long wait in a line that snaked back through the paint section in six-foot intervals, Richard now drove out of the parking lot past the curb where the day laborers lingered, the Mexicans and Central Americans who lived eight to a house in the rundown neighborhoods, pulling weeds and painting garages by day and half-sleeping through the night, waiting for the knock on the door from ICE. Only two men stood at the curb. One of them tried to make eye contact with drivers as they exited. The other guy was white, maybe in his mid-twenties. Richard had never seen a white man at this exit before, an area usually reserved only for brown bodies. He wore overalls, a hoodie, a rain jacket, work boots, and a knapsack. Attached to it were a hard hat and a thick coiled rope that looked strong enough to tow a freighter. There was talk of construction projects throughout the country being forced to shut down, and this young man had the look of somebody who, minutes before, had been laid off by the company building the apartments across the street. Richard was momentarily transfixed by the sight of this strapping, good-looking kid, standing straight with his chin proudly jutting, like he was posing for a billboard advertising hardworking Real White Americans, waiting for someone to realize how lucky they were to find such a rare specimen of manly brawn on this undignified patch of sidewalk. Perhaps he needed money for the bus back home, or for a motel room to avoid the close quarters of a shelter, or maybe for the lunch he forgot to pack. His presence was unsettling. It seemed to confirm that things were coming unmoored in the country and no one was noticing the small ruptures. All over the United States, the formerly employed were at loose ends, standing in place, wondering where to turn.

5

WATCHING

"If you see me going numb," Beth said, dropping their Trader Joe's tortellini into the boiling water, "tell me."

She could behave that way in a crisis. Frozen in place in a kind of temporary catatonia. Usually she snapped out of it, but he knew what she was getting at. Beth and Chloe had been robbed at knifepoint while hiking in Oaxaca in December. The man who accosted them was thin, dressed in dirty clothes, visibly anxious, holding a steak knife. Beth shut down. Things moved in slow motion. She handed over pesos and her phone, waiting for the robber to make the next move. But Chloe, her own phone concealed in an interior pocket, emptied her entire day pack on the ground, showing they had nothing else of value, stuffed everything back into her pack, and then grabbed her mother's arm. "Que tenga buen dia!" she said with sarcastic anger, as they bolted down the hill.

"I don't want to go numb during any of this," Beth said, "Don't let me."

What would that look like? Well, for starters, taking an overly optimistic view of the situation. Beth was not really a Pollyanna, but she did always try to look on the bright side. Sometimes they'd clashed over this. He'd prefer the grimmer view of things and claim he was only being "realistic." If she refused to read any bad news, this would mean her head was going in the sand. If she remained cheerful even after the store shelves emptied and the water and power were shut off, this would be worrying. If she continued to believe the Democrats were going to take back the government despite impending martial law, the suspension of elections, a ban on protests and the arrests of newspaper publishers, this would be what one could call going numb. If, after watching the managing editor of NPR executed live on Fox News, she then returned to listening to opera through her earbuds while downloading recipes from the *New York Times*, he would know that shock had set in.

During their election night party four years ago, as he and a few other masochists remained flayed in glum mute postures across the couch and the ottomans, staring motionless at the CNN map as the malignancy spread through Michigan, Wisconsin, and Pennsylvania, Beth walked into the room in a pantsuit and started taking pictures with a smile on her face, still believing in miracles and uncounted votes, unable to align the grotesque reality of the night with her long-dreamed wish for a female president. She laughed about it later, when they could laugh a little again.

"I don't think you'll go numb," he said. "I won't let that happen."

They loaded up their plates with the tortellini and pancetta and walked the few feet from their kitchen through their backyard and into his studio to watch the news. A contractor had converted their garage into an office and home cinema room, installing heat, electrical outlets, flooring, windows, sheetrock, and soundproofing. Richard painted the room in Caribbean blue, red, and orange. He paid a thousand bucks for a sixty-two-inch plasma screen with deep blacks and wide dynamic range, bought a Blu-ray player and a surround sound audio system, lined the walls with film posters in foreign languages. Il Cacciatore, *The Deer Hunter*. Soy Cuba, *I Am Cuba*. Il Caso Thomas Crown, *The Thomas Crown Affair*.

This is where he edited their videos, where he wrote and compiled playlists for his radio program, where he spent hours watching films. Esoteric offerings from the streaming sites, and auteurist masterworks from his growing collection of DVDs and Blu-rays: the complete works of Bergman and Cassavetes, Antonioni's brilliant films of alienation, Mizoguchi's black-and-white studies of female oppression, Bela Tarr's eight-hour *Satantango*. Richard imagined that one day the internet would overload and crash, and people would have to relearn the ancient technologies, the manual placement of a thin plastic disc into a pop-out tray in a player, the tray sliding back in, the information on the disc decoded into sound and light, arising from the depths of the black screen like an act of necromancy. This was an endangered species, a film you could hold in your hands.

He scrolled through the on-screen options until he found the CBS Evening News. With its two-minute packages, its rapid-fire cutting and reporter standups, the show would provide a quick overview of the day's events, images to back up the clipped reports they got from NPR. The anchorman announced that viewer discretion was advised.

Beth and Richard put down their forks, clutched their glasses of wine, and watched in mute alarm: gasping bodies laid out in the corridors of a Madrid hospital. A funeral home full of coffins in Lombardy. Ambulances wailing through deserted Manhattan streets. Pleading nurses in Brooklyn. Long lines of silent people at food banks. Video from Wuhan showing a young man screaming as he was dragged off to quarantine by helmeted soldiers.

The virus had subsumed everything. The planet was in its thrall.

Wars stopped. The border wall abandoned in mid-rivet. Asylum claims put on permanent hold. People with cancer? Get in line. Need an abortion? Not this pregnancy.

Everyone, it had to be admitted, was numb. A virus the size of a fraction of an eyelash had laid waste to the world economy within two weeks, trapped people in their homes and apartments, cleared highways of traffic, brought the world to heel. It was beginning to dawn on humanity that the contagion was in control, and a quick end to the pandemic did not seem likely.

Was this really the end of days? Was it really happening? Richard had always imagined he would observe the apocalypse from afar, filmed through a telephoto lens, with a slow pan across a burning horizon, maybe with a rack focus from a smoldering minivan to a chopper lifting off in the smoky distance. He believed he would somehow emerge unscathed, like a Marvel character, with stories to tell of epic scope and heroism. But he hadn't figured on a virus, something unseen and inviolate vaulting to the top of the food chain, consigning him to a ventilator in a hospital, surrounded by ghostly figures in PPE, his family out of reach, unable to touch or see him, as his breathing receded and his organs shut down one by one, like the turning off of house lights.

The U.S. now totaled 100,000 cases, more than any other country.

Health workers were being sickened by the dozens in the five New York boroughs.

A ship with five hundred beds departed a Virginia naval yard for Manhattan.

Field hospitals were constructed in parking lots.

A refrigerated truck sat at a loading dock outside an overflowing morgue.

Triage. Ventilator. Coffin.
    Supply chains. Lockdown. Anosmia.
    Comorbidity. Trenches. Field hospitals.
    Refrigerated trucks.

Meanwhile, the president bellowed, "I want to see the pews full for Easter Sunday!"

Zach's condition had improved. He said he was able to come over for dinner. Richard looked forward to seeing his son but this meant that all day long he was distracted by a continual hum of panic. Sometimes it seemed audible, like tinnitus, an incoming tide of white noise washing into the gullies of his day, making it difficult to sustain concentration on any one task for more than twenty minutes at a time. He wasn't sure if his panic was situational, caused by the possibility of his son bringing the pathogen into their house, or if it was global, signaled by the blinking engine light of his own insignificance. He was in a perpetual state of waiting for the next smothering wave to wash over him.

Beth placed a dispenser of homemade hand sanitizer near the front door. Another in the bathroom. She set a spray bottle of bleach and paper towels on the counter. Richard took a tape measure into the living room, marking off six feet between where Zach would sit and where he and Beth and Chloe would sit, creating an invisible DMZ between themselves and their own child.

Zach arrived, waving to them from the doorway, and Richard pointed him to a chair on one side of the living room and they sat on the other. Drinks on side tables. Plates on their laps. Their living room window open to a chilly breeze. They all felt it was possible to distance themselves indoors just enough for it not to feel too awkward, this one-act play of a family meal. Zach said he was feeling a lot better, and he looked and sounded good, with his humor intact, although his sense of smell still seemed a little off.

"How are you both doing?" Richard asked, looking first at Chloe and then at Zach. "I mean, you know, emotionally?"

"Pretty good," said Zach. "Bummed about not being able to see anyone. Bummed about being stuck in my little room at Carol's." Carol was the woman who owned the house where he rented a room the size of a screened porch for $650 a month, with a toilet down the hall, and a few shelves in the kitchen assigned to him where he stacked his Ethiopian grind and packages of Top Ramen. Carol, in her late sixties, was terrified of catching the virus, so she made Zach wash every item he brought home from the store, including the fruit and vegetables, and she prohibited him from having his girlfriend over.

"I'm glad I've got a place to go to, honestly, thanks to you guys," said Chloe, looking at her parents. "Some of my friends in Missoula aren't able to go home. They've been alone for two weeks." All of her graduate courses and teaching responsibilities had shifted online. "But, honestly? I don't know how much longer I can do this."

"You're talking about the online thing?" Beth asked.

"Yeah, I mean, I've been looking at my laptop for seven hours a day. I fucking hate it."

"You guys will tell us if you start, you know, feeling wigged out, or you get depressed?" Richard asked. "I mean, it's okay to be depressed, this is fucked up, but make sure you talk to us if it gets to be too much."

"I'm okay," Zach said. "At least I can go for walks, and I'm starting to work on my film again."

"Yeah, getting out for a run is important," said Chloe. "At least we can do that."

Richard was also trying to go for runs, or jogs, actually, which more accurately described his pace. Despite a healthy pulse, the stamina to tackle backcountry hikes and urban stairs, and a good cholesterol reading (an *impressive* HDL, his doctor had told him, but that was six years ago), he had still gained weight in the last few years. Even though he ate the Mediterranean diet—olive oil, nuts, fish, leafy greens—and usually skipped the middle aisles of the grocery store, his flesh had somehow mutated into a topo map of his indulgences. An unwillingness to cut down on his intake of beer and wine, along with the slowing metabolism of his age, cancelled out the calories he burned while exercising. He consoled himself with the idea that in times of catastrophe—a famine, say, or a plane crash in the Andes—the survivors were often the heaviest, living off the fat of their own bodies until the rescue team arrived, while the marathon runner or the lifelong calorie-counter were the first to perish, full of regret for the brownies and the oatmeal stouts they'd passed up. He secretly hoped that new medical research would reveal exercise actually *shortened* lives, inexorably grinding bones to dust, sapping residual energies, shaving minutes off longevity with each squat thrust. Doctors would suddenly advise everyone to stop exercising immediately and commit to a program of daytime drinking.

"They're already talking about coming up with a vaccine," Beth said, in her hopeful way.

"Yeah, but they're saying it will take two years," Richard said.

"Do you remember," Beth said, turning to him, "our typhoid shots?"

This was back in the late eighties, when they were preparing for their honeymoon, a backpacking trip around the world, starting with marriage in Scotland at a one-thousand-year-old church. Neither of them was Scottish, but the country didn't require a residency period before getting hitched, and they thought it would be exciting to start their life together in a foreign country and then spend the next ten months traveling through Europe, Morocco, India, Nepal, Malaysia, Java, Thailand, Singapore, Australia. They received the typhoid shots on a drizzly September morning and then celebrated with a Hangtown Fry at Lowell's in Pike Place Market. Two hours later, back in Beth's apartment, they were both shaking uncontrollably, huddling under blankets like Sid and Nancy. They had a touch of typhoid, exactly what the nurse had said. They recovered within an hour. The shots were good for ten years.

"What about you guys?" Chloe asked. "How are *you* holding up?"

"I'm okay," Beth said. "Yes, being able to get outside and exercise is kind of saving me. I'm feeling okay with the Zoom thing. I started talking to the Wellesley girls." She was, after forty years, still friends with the women she roomed with in college, all of them scattered around the country. Richard was envious of her friendships. For twenty years, he'd played gym-rat basketball with a group of guys, but stopped because he was afraid of snapping an Achilles or tearing an ACL. They never saw each other off the court. There was his friend Anthony, who lived in Seattle, and another friend in Kansas City and another in London. These were the only men he talked to semi-regularly.

"I don't know. I'm alright," he said. "Taking really long walks, trying to run a little, watching films. It's like—" He paused, not sure how far he wanted to take this. "It's like, how much more fucked up can things get. I feel like we're all sort of on our own, on the edge of a kind of lawlessness. Things could get ugly." He stopped there. Chloe's question was meant to be a kind of check-in, not an invitation to full disclosure. He didn't want to burden his children with his issues. Besides, what did he have to disclose? He wasn't debilitated. He still got out of bed in the morning. He had an appetite. He managed to walk several miles a day and he found comfort in revisiting his favorite films: *Heat. Point Break. Salvador. To Live and Die in L.A.*

"I'm okay though," he said, quickly. "I just want to make sure you all are okay."

They finished dinner, made a few jokes, air kissed. Zach stood at the door and waved. Then he drove away through the soundless streets.

For the last ten years, Richard would retreat alone to his studio in the pre-dawn hours and watch films. He kept the blinds down and the lights off. Something he'd read, saw, heard, ate, would remind him of a movie and he would have an urgent desire to see it again. A plate of bucatini all'Amatriciana would lead him to Fellini's *La Dolce Vita*. A drive through an Eastern Washington wheat field and he'd watch Malick's *Days of Heaven* for the umpteenth time. Two mornings ago, he saw photos of the crowd on Bourbon Street—the sandwiched bodies like one heaving undulant host for the virus—and decided to check out Elia Kazan's *Panic in the Streets*, a fast-paced noir about an outbreak of pneumonic plague in New Orleans. The actor Richard Widmark—whose face always seemed vaguely amphibious—starred as a Department of National Health specialist, schooled in the protocols of masks, gloves, and quarantine. The film played on the tension between the federal government and the city's police, with Widmark and a local cop racing against time to find a murderous thug infected with the lethal contagion, ending in a foot chase under the city's grimy docks and wharves. The thug dead. The pathogen contained.

This morning, the film was Antonioni's *Blow-Up*. "Nothing like a little disaster for sorting things out," says the protagonist, the fashion photographer whose desire to make a difference with his work, to take pictures of more than pretty clothes and the pretty things inside them, leads him to believe he's witnessed a murder. Or, Antonioni asks, is he only trying to convince himself he saw something that never occurred? Perhaps the optimal choice, Richard concluded, is to live in a state of ignorant bliss, to be unconcerned with the tension between responsibility and oblivion.

This watching, sitting alone, sipping his coffee, hypnotized by a Kurosawa or a Godard, was a kind of practice, a meditation, a ritual of self-care. He was bound to his cinephiliac obsessions, and he knew that it bred a sort of smugness. He disdained the predictable, the mass-produced, the heavily advertised, the over-saturated. He could sometimes tolerate conventional set-ups in the films he watched as long as they were rendered with the skew of a singular intelligence, but he was easily bored by conventions in prestige television, popular music, and bestsellers, especially the mass-marketed pseudo-philosophical semi-fantasies that ran 600 pages or more. As a rule, he didn't like long books—he never read Proust and he never made it out of the boarding house in *Moby-Dick*—but he did read Knausgaard's epic six-volume work, *My Struggle*, 3,600 pages total in paperback. The books were stacked in the living room on a shelf under the stereo, visible to guests, like a monument to his erudition.

For the most part, Richard tried to keep his snobbery in check. Among Seattle's liberals (they were *everywhere*), there was an ongoing public display of self-satisfied virtue signaling (in almost *everything*, from plastic bags to pronouns) that annoyed him. He would gripe to Beth about the minefield of political correctness they had to tiptoe through when dealing with their clients. Once, as an experiment, he considered self-identifying as queer in order to qualify for a grant.

The efforts to keep up exhausted him. Sometimes he could understand the red-state rubes who laughed at the blue-state snowflakes. After all, his lifestyle was just as easy to lampoon—with his taste for Mosaic hops and transgressive cinema—as the gender-fluid first-grade teacher with a doggy backpack.

He slid *Blow-Up* back into its sleeve, raised the blinds, and tried to get some work done.

Their only steady client—in addition to Shelley, whom he had taken to calling The Heiress—was an arts organization that brought local writers into schools and paid renowned authors a tidy sum to lecture at well-attended public readings. He combed through the footage they'd shot in the months before the pandemic. Interviews Beth conducted with students. B-roll of them writing and reading poetry. The imaginative inner worlds of the sixth graders moved him; the ability of high schoolers to channel pain and politics into personal works of outrage and commentary inspired him. Reading and writing were still viable pursuits, he was happy to see, but they had to compete with pointless distractions like Snapchat and TikTok.

Almost as a reflex, Richard checked the ranking of his book on Amazon. Number 1,592,408 in the universal category, number 320 in the category of Documentary Movies. For a very brief few weeks a year ago, he was in the category's top thirty, at number 28, but that anemic glow of fame quickly dissolved as his book slid back down to number 53, then 185, and then into obscurity. He'd saddled it with the title *Get Close: Lean Team Documentary Filmmaking*, which was now an ironic joke, since nobody was allowed to get close to anything. He was still proud that he'd written it, and the editor who accepted his proposal thought it had a future.

That was two years ago, on the morning before Richard was due to fly to Paris for a film festival. He received an email from Oxford University Press, one of the four publishers where he'd sent his query:

Dear Richard,

My thanks for this. I've had a chance to read this afternoon — the timing proved to be perfect as the reading could accompany me on some train travels — and I can offer some reactions. Overall this is a good thing. You are an expert filmmaker and you are seeking to equip junior generations with time-tested tools for making documentaries. And the writing wears its wisdom lightly, exactly as I would hope for the audiences you wish to reach.

Naturally, the elation Richard felt upon reading this was quickly dulled by what he knew would happen next. He would be ghosted, the new passive-aggressive method of rejection, once the editor discovered he lacked an advanced degree and that his sample chapters contained an avalanche of grammatical oddities. In order to get it over with, he came clean right away, telling the editor he didn't have a master's and that this was his first book and . . . it didn't matter. The editor preferred his conversational tone and real-world experience to the academic praxis (whatever the fuck that word meant) that he usually had to hack his way through.

So, two days later, there Richard was in his Parisian studio, a one-room rented garret in Montmartre, down the hill from Sacré Cœur, fine-tuning the proposal before submitting it for approval to the OUP contract board. He worked on the book in the mornings and then walked ten miles every day among the arrondissements, stopping at galleries and museums and expensive stationery stores. He indulged in long lunches with a book and a glass of Sauvignon at sidewalk tables on the Île Saint-Louis, late-afternoon espressos and reading in the Marais, Pâtes aux Lardons and a carafe of Bordeaux on the Rue des Abbesses for dinner.

Beth had joined him there on her way back from a trip to China. They found an outside table at a crowded bistro and sat with heaters and blankets and watched the people go by. She lapped up the melted gruyere from a bowl of French onion soup. He ate roast chicken and potatoes. She drank from a half-carafe of airy rosé, he from a half-carafe of burgundy. The next day they watched their latest documentary, a film about a clinic in a poor Peruvian suburb, screen to a small audience in a sweltering and airless basement cinema.

It depressed him to think about it now. Paris. The book. How long before any of the world's great cities could open again? If we remain alive but the virus kills all of our joys, what will be the upside? He kept Paris in the weather app on his phone. He liked to swipe to it, see a week of bright suns, and fall into a daydream of spending April in Paris, set to the Charlie Parker version of the song. But now, the suns mocked the abandoned cafés and desolate museums, the vacant bars and cinemas, and the poor Parisians quarantined in their tiny Haussmann apartments.

The mechanical groan of a garbage truck reverberated outside his studio window. He had forgotten to put out their trash and compost, so he clicked out of Amazon, walked through his backyard, and dragged the bins into the alley. There was Abdul down the street, twisting a socket wrench and getting ready to duck under the hood of a car. Abdul motioned him over.

"This is very bad!" Abdul said, frowning.

Richard stopped six feet away. "It's scary, I know. Are you and your family okay?"

Abdul was married and had two kids. He was a shade tree mechanic, fixing cars belonging to his Muslim neighbors, although there weren't any trees to provide shade over the parking spaces where he worked. They'd first talked years ago, shortly after he and Beth moved in. Abdul had told him to watch out for the local teenagers.

"Criminals! Very bad. They have guns!" He'd mimicked holding a gun in his hand.

At the time, there was a group of young Muslim men and boys who wandered the streets and gathered near the park. Loud shouts late in the night. Territorial battles. Frequent calls to 911. The Muslim mothers were as concerned as everyone else. Things came to a head two years later, the teens opening up with AR-15s in an alley on a summer day, children leaping from tire swings and ducking for cover. One of the shooters was quickly arrested. Turns out his father was running an illegal luxury car service, buying up broken-down Maseratis and Porsches from police auctions, and letting the unlicensed youth drive them at high speeds through the twenty-mile-an-hour streets. The family was evicted and gradually New Rainier Vista settled into the tranquil multicultural quilt the brochures had advertised.

He and Abdul never delved too deeply into each other's lives when they chatted. Early on, Abdul wanted to be sure Richard agreed with him that the youth were not to be coddled, and later, after the election, Abdul wanted to be sure Richard agreed with him that the new president was obviously a cartoonish—but dangerous—dictator-in-waiting. He and his wife were Vietnamese Muslims, having fled persecution a few years after the war ended. Abdul knew a thing or two about tyrants and repression.

One day, when Richard was loading up the trunk of their car with camping gear, Abdul came over and asked if they were moving.

"Nope. We're just going camping for a few nights."

"Camping? You sleep in a tent?" He looked concerned.

"Yeah! We love it. It's nice to be outside in the summer. Have you ever camped?"

Abdul peered into the trunk as if it were a grave.

"Yes. Four years we lived in a refugee camp in Cambodia, sleeping in tents all the time. I will never do that again."

Now, Abdul wanted to be sure Richard agreed with him that the current crisis was, indeed, very bad.

"People dying. And that man, he does nothing. He is crazy. People sick. He does nothing. Lying all the time."

"I know, it's awful. We can't listen to him. There are people trying to help. Are you able to stay home? Stay safe? You'll be okay?"

"Yes. Yes. Okay here. But I'm very worried."

"Yes. Me, too."

Later that day, the Centers for Disease Control announced that all Americans should wear masks, after weeks in which everyone was told they didn't need to wear them. Suddenly, mask-making tutorials popped up on Facebook and YouTube. A person could sew a mask from a scrap of T-shirt or quickly fold a bandanna into a makeshift version. Within a day it seemed everyone in Seattle now carried a mask with them—the good old-fashioned American can-do spirit in action—but Richard wondered how many people could have avoided getting sick if they were told to make their own masks earlier, much earlier, in the first weeks of February, before the contagion took hold. Did the CDC tell people they didn't need a mask because they were worried that all of the available masks for hospital workers would be hoarded by some amoral opportunist? Or had the toddler in the Oval Office so infantilized the population that nobody in a position of authority felt they could trust the public to understand a simple directive? (Richard had actually never agreed with the characterization of the president as a toddler. After all, toddlers can be trained to listen, to learn, to look at the world around them and find ways to navigate, to get along, to make friends, to grow. They have fits of course, terrible tantrums and episodes of obstinate refusal, but they ultimately want to be liked, to be loved, and to give love back. They eventually evolve into compassionate human beings. No, the president was definitely not a toddler).

Beth rinsed lettuce, he brushed olive oil on salmon, and Chloe sliced tomatoes. At thirty years old, she hadn't planned on spending months living in her parents' townhome and eating dinner with them every night. But she would come to the kitchen in good spirits, sometimes with a short video to share from her phone. One featured a pair of doctors singing "Imagine." Another, an older couple sitting at their dining room table in Chicago crooning their novelty version of "Homeward Bound." There was something sweet about these bits of homemade entertainment, an attempt to find a tender solidarity within their predicament, to ward off the dreariness for a few minutes, a dreariness so tactile that it seemed to possess bulk and bearing. This collective bonhomie wouldn't last much longer, Richard predicted. In the first week or two of lockdown, people in the cities had gathered on their balconies or front lawns and banged pots and pans in support of doctors and nurses. The housebound placed teddy bears in their windows for children to discover as they walked the streets with their parents. Eventually these activities faded, as the grueling reality enervated the waking hours.

Later that evening the three of them watched Robert Altman's *Nashville*, a film that Richard had first seen in high school and at least ten times since. The fictitious presidential candidate, Hal Philip Walker, is heard but never seen, his voice blaring from a loudspeaker attached to the top of a van constantly roving the streets. He calls for a disruption of the status quo. An end to politics and politicians. An overthrow of the tax system. Protection for the rights of workers. Some of his statements make sense, speaking for the citizens of a palsied country shaking off the Nixon years. Walker's party is called the Replacement Party. His handlers believe if they can get the leading lights of country music to support him, they will win over the forgotten man, America's silent majority. Their cynical ploy ends with an assassination of one of the doyens of country music during her comeback concert. She is carried from the stage in her bloodied white dress as the audience rises up to sing the movie's anthem: "It Don't Worry Me."

Was there still a place for the righteous assassination? Historically, assassins mostly succeeded in killing the fearless and the inspirational. Lincoln, Gandhi, King, the Kennedys. The kinds of leaders in short supply nowadays. Some tyrants—Hussein, Ghaddafi, Ceaușescu—were first caught and then executed, but many of history's most ruthless oppressors and architects of genocide avoided assassination, eventually dying hackneyed deaths in dachas and villas and bunkers: Stalin, cerebral hemorrhage. Papa Doc Duvalier, heart disease and diabetes. Idi Amin, kidneys. Pol Pot, heart failure. Hitler, suicide.

Now, whenever he heard the president bathe himself in a slurry of lies and resentments and insults, blaming others for the carnage sweeping the land, Richard daydreamed of assassination. The president seemed more intrigued with the high TV ratings of his briefings than he did with the deaths of American citizens. He compared his numbers to those for Monday Night Football and *The Bachelor*, and then wondered how the mainstream press could ignore this obvious evidence of his popularity. "They all hate me," he complained, with his obtuse talent for making self-pity a point of pride.

Hard Times in Babylon

The doctor who led the medical section of the administration's coronavirus task force had convinced the president to backtrack on his call for his true believers to fill the church pews. She apparently had presented him with colorful charts and graphs illustrating the heaps of bodies that would be stacked on the White House lawn if he didn't change his tune. The doctor appeared at the virus press briefings draped in elaborate patterned scarves, a sartorial effect that seemed to clash with the grave business at hand. Maybe the doctor or another one of the cardboard cutouts who stood behind the president on the podium during his daily vaudeville show would finally get fed up with his moronic rantings. Perhaps the Surgeon General, the guy in the Captain Kangaroo outfit, would extract a shiv from an inside pocket and efficiently insert it into the base of the president's skull. The blood would splatter the Captain's epaulets and spurt across the crash test dummy's fawning smile and splash the doctor's scarves, her shock giving way to sudden relief when it dawned on her she would no longer have to humiliate herself by attaching a faux coherence to her boss's unhinged ramblings. The president would collapse onto the lectern and then tumble forward into the lap of his favorite reporter from One America News, his liar's blood oozing into the red Vicuna wool of her dress. The cameras would continue to roll, a reporter from the liberal media would issue a short burst of applause, someone out of frame would say, audible to the world, *Thank God.*

This fantasy extended to a different, darker corner of Richard's thoughts: He was contemplating buying a gun, something he'd never seriously thought about before. But now he imagined the three ways a gun might come in handy. Yes, assassination, but also self-defense and, you know, the other thing. Assassination would be logistically difficult and, frankly, kind of absurd. In no way could Richard picture himself as some kind of Okay Boomer version of Lee Harvey Oswald. He wasn't really the stand-your-ground type either. An act of self-defense would require him to have the stomach to actually point the gun at someone, issue a threat, and then follow through with pulling the trigger. As for suicide, he'd read plenty of articles about how having a gun in the house made it easier to kill oneself, and this frightened him at a core level. But he also believed he should at least learn how to shoot one of the things; it seemed like everyone in the zombie shows he watched, *The Walking Dead* and *Black Summer,* from grandmothers to little boys, instinctively knew how to hold and fire a weapon. He started googling local gun shops and ranges to see if any had yet reopened. He bookmarked the sites, setting an alert on his calendar to check back in a few weeks.

6

NUMBERS

The days continued to play out, one after the other, an endless roulette, where people did not place bets or speak of odds but merely watched the wheel spin slowly and stop on another number.

Digital maps showed the virus beginning to level off ever so slightly on the West Coast and along the New England seaboard, in the states that were the first to mandate social distancing, to close bars and schools, to ask people to shelter in place, to encourage mask wearing. This hopeful news was signified on the maps by a light brown or gray color, soothing earth tones representing a flattening of the infection curve. But in the unruly swath of states across the country's vast middle and south, the uptick in deaths and infections among the president's foot soldiers was represented by a throb of orange-red, like a mass of suppurating tissue. Finally, the president issued a solemn press statement on the wearing of masks, although he insisted this was entirely voluntary, and that he certainly wasn't going to wear one himself because, well, that would look ridiculous, especially while greeting all of the presidents and prime ministers from other countries, all the dictators and kings and queens and knights and fairies and elves who clamored to meet with him.

. . .

Wrapped in a blanket against the pre-dawn chill, Richard sat on his back porch reading, waiting for the sun to pink the charcoal sky. Their neighborhood was in the flight path, and he had complained last year to Beth that the roar of planes never seemed to stop, the intervals between jets growing shorter and shorter, more landings and takeoffs than when they first moved to the townhome nine years ago. But now, with the majority of flights cancelled, he could better hear the barking dog, the seagulls screeching as they were chased by crows, the oscillation of tiny wings as a hummingbird briefly hovered near the bamboo planter. He could better hear the purr of ambient music from his portable speaker. The sustained pulsing drones and the digitized loops and repetitions seemed to emanate from the ocean floor.

Next door lived a couple with two young kids, a boy and a girl. The parents had decided to separate in February, but the pandemic stalled their plans. Now they argued, their shouts cracking the quiet, something about shoes stacked outside the back door, although a marital argument is rarely about the thing they are yelling about. They eventually stopped shouting, or they took it deeper inside away from their open windows.

He tried to concentrate on his book, rereading, for the third time, Don DeLillo's *White Noise*, but the distractions kept piling up. Squirrels emerged from under the eaves on the garage roof and scampered down the tree trunks. Two cars drag-raced on an empty MLK. He grabbed his phone and began researching prices on revolvers. Guns-R-Us, eBay, Craigslist. Everywhere, guns. This was better than doing nothing, better than just sitting where he was, poring over his past mistakes, the missed opportunities, and the roads not taken.

The freeze-dried food and rain pants were delivered to their doorstep in a large cardboard box, the delivery driver ringing the doorbell and walking away. Here was something else to take Richard's mind off of himself. He ripped through the acres of packaging, gathered the foiled pouches of food together in tote bags and placed the bags into a plastic bin, along with their canisters of butane, water filters, plastic bowls, an emergency wind-up flashlight, a battery-powered lantern, toilet paper, paper towels, and bear spray. Next on his to-do list was to gather his hiking outfit (quick-dry shorts and underwear and T-shirt and light wool socks), along with a hat, gloves, sleeping bag, sleeping pad, tent, trekking poles, sunscreen, mosquito repellent, head lamp, emergency blanket, waterproof matches, and Swiss Army knife. He asked Beth to assemble a first aid kit from the odds and ends they had around the house. He made sure to have an extra backpack, sleeping bag, pad, and tent for Zach. They'd collected enough camping gear over the years to see them through for ten days, maybe two weeks, before their fuel and food would run out. Chloe, the now-seasoned backcountry trail-crew leader, was already outfitted. She suggested they always keep their gas tanks topped off. Their water bottles filled. Their escape routes mapped. Their rendezvous points coordinated. Her boyfriend lived in a small town off a highway in the Cascade Mountains, on a piece of land next to the Skykomish River, which exploded out of the mountains every spring like a jailbreak. Maybe they could hole up there.

That afternoon David and James, neighbors from across the park, came over for drinks. Richard and Beth sat with them in the alley behind their house, where the sun stayed out longer before descending behind the greenbelt bordering the neighborhood. They spaced their lawn chairs six feet apart and grouped mixed nuts into two separate bowls and served them on personal side tables. David preferred twenty-ounce cans of IPA and James brought along two tumblers of his favorite cocktail, a Negroni.

"I'm going to end up being known as the old queen wandering aimlessly around the neighborhood every evening slurping his Negroni," James said.

David, the quieter of the two, was retired from Microsoft. He was a recent cancer survivor and had to be particularly watchful against the virus. James was a photographer who'd recently mounted an exhibit of his work. It had opened on the same day that nearly everyone in the city began to recognize the severity of the contagion. The gallery shut down three days later.

"I was planning on going to your show when I got back from Georgia," Richard said.

"We were going to come that Saturday," Beth started to say.

"And it was cancelled on Friday. I know. My first-ever exhibit."

"Over before it really got started," muttered David.

"Damn," added Richard, commiserating. "I had three screenings planned of the film about my mother, for that local series, called Meaningful Movies. I'd been emailing with them for months to set this up. And then, poof."

"It's okay," James said. "I mean, I would have liked to go through with the show, but this is happening everywhere, not just to me."

"I don't even want to think about all the artists, all the freelancers," Beth said, shaking her head. "How are they going to make a living?"

"Restaurants shutting down," David said. "I imagine a lot of actors and dancers still work as waiters."

"They're fucked," said James.

"We all might be fucked," Richard added.

David swallowed the last of his first IPA and opened his second.

"I don't want to think of myself as a senior citizen," David said. "But I like that the PCC has early hours for seniors."

"And pregnant women," James added.

"And the, what is it," Richard said, elaborating the syllables, "immun-o-compro-mised?"

"I'm happy to call myself a senior citizen if it means fewer people in the store," Beth said.

"I like it. Forces me out of the house at six a.m. I feel fairly safe," said David. "As long as I keep the avocados between me and anyone else."

"And, I guess now, we have our masks," Beth added.

"Are we supposed to report people not wearing their masks," Richard asked, "point at them accusingly, give them dirty looks?" He mimicked a loudspeaker: "*Tech bro spotted without mask on aisle five. Commence extermination procedure.*"

They wondered if they should wear surgical gloves while shopping.

"Can the virus stick to a glove or only to your hands?" Beth asked.

"Who the fuck knows," said James.

"No one knows anything at this point," said David.

They all agreed that the virus would probably ease up in a month, if they just followed the rules, practiced patience. After an hour in the alley, the sun dropped behind the trees and the air chilled. They made plans to meet up again next week.

The weather took two steps back. Rain and cold returned. The sky dark as graphite. The governor extended the stay-at-home orders well into May. There was a collective gritting of teeth throughout the state, a growing claustrophobia, the insistent murmur of desperation, as the numbers kept multiplying.

Four-thirty in the morning. Saturday. Richard got up, after lying awake for forty-five minutes listening to Zoomie calling from the front porch. They'd had their cat for fourteen years. His fur was black, with the rich luster of a vinyl LP. He had long stiff white whiskers, and a meow that expressed a symphony of moods. He spent the spring and summer months outside at night, patrolling the perimeter, leaving snapped-neck trophies on the front and back steps. Mice and voles and baby rats. They knew about the statistics regarding outdoor cats killing off songbirds, but Zoomie seemed to prefer wingless game. His proper name was Zoom. Sometimes they referred to him as The Zoomster, or Furball, or Fuzzy, or His Majesty. It was unfortunate that their cat bore the same name as the video-conferencing app sweeping the nation. Zoom the cat was so much more limber and responsive than Zoom the app.

Richard fed him, made the coffee, left a thermos out for Beth, and retreated to his studio, where he struggled through a morning viewing of Fellini's *La Strada*, a film he remembered fondly, especially for its tragic finale. This time, though, he found Anthony Quinn's irredeemable, one-trick circus performer an unpleasant bore, and he could only muster a glimmer of empathy for Giulietta Masina's doormat simpleton of a character. But when the ending arrived, he couldn't help but be moved again by Quinn's anguished cry to the night stars, a howl of perpetual loneliness, a stab to the heart. He'd abandoned Masina years before, and then learned she had died a vagabond. "What do I have now that I cast aside the only person who ever loved me?" Quinn's character asks, resigned to a future of unremitting solitude.

Forty degrees. A breeze snapping up from the south. Richard worked the film over in his mind as he walked along the Chief Sealth trail on the hill above their neighborhood, Sealth being the Duwamish Indian for whom Seattle was named. He was a peacemaker, skilled at oratory, famous for his spirited, wise epigraphs, often misquoted or apocryphal: *Man does not weave this web of life. He is merely a strand of it. Whatever he does to the web, he does to himself.*

The trail snaked for miles along a high ridge dotted with power lines and scored by a bike path that ran up and down between the housing projects and the community pea patches and the four-bedroom homes where people had to walk up a flight of interior stairs before the living could begin. The foothills of the Cascades lumped to the east, the mouth of the Duwamish river opening to Puget Sound to the west, and there, over his right shoulder as he walked south, the Olympics again, like a billboard drawing you into its promise of summer hiking and camping.

The streaming channel on his iPhone emitted a shoe-gazing electronica. Not his usual diet, but it fit his black mood. He walked with his head down, distracted by the whispers in his mind, the whispers that woke him an hour before he got out of bed, the whispers of despair. This was encyclopedic despair, despair on an interplanetary level. Forget himself, or his neighborhood, or the city, what about the rest of the world? He'd read a news story from Ecuador, with pictures of corpses strewn in alleys, and thought about the work he and Beth had done in Bangladesh and El Salvador and Peru, crafting short films on clean water projects and gardening initiatives for NGOs, interviewing doctors tracking genetic diseases like Parkinson's and Huntington's, shooting high-definition video of students in gleaming new rural schools. Many of these people still lived crowded into slums, makeshift sprawls where thousands of tin-sided shacks were accordioned together, families living inches apart. What would happen if these places were overtaken by the contagion? Would the dead be left to decompose in sewage ditches?

He tried to fight against it, this despair, but another, more troubling feeling had wormed its way forward: futility. The futility of believing things would eventually improve, for himself, for his family, for the world at large. He had never been a practitioner of the great American passion for positive thinking, the unquestioned belief in their nation's exceptionalism, in the inventions and innovations and technologies that would save them from international terrorism and climate chaos, from invading armies and invading pathogens. He believed positive thinking was a special type of American disease, a kind of blindness that obscured the truth of things.

Turning east, he walked down toward the southern end of MLK, to a stretch that featured Ethiopian restaurants, hair-extension shops, cannabis stores, payday lenders, mini-marts, and more nail salons. Businesses were locked behind iron grates, trash blowing through the bars and piling up in the doorways. There was one lone pedestrian, a young man dressed in the layered clothing of the homeless, looking either menacing or maybe just ill. Another empty train clattered past. It was as if the End Times were on an accelerated timetable here, only two miles south of his neighborhood. The area had struggled for years to attract millennial renters and the cohort of fusion restaurants, microbreweries, and pour-over coffee bars that followed. Even low-wage bohemians, the pioneers of gentrification, hadn't quite gained a toehold.

Back in Columbia City, he stopped again at the bakery. But the doors were now locked and there was a sign on the window: *We hoped to remain open, but for the safety and convenience of our workers we have reluctantly closed our doors. We have 24 employees.*

Twenty-four employees. No doubt all of them were attempting to file for unemployment, spending hours on websites that were clogged or crashing, online systems apparently built on obsolete software from floppy disks, understood only by long-retired engineers now living in condos near ski resorts. No one knew how to reconfigure the pipes to get the money flowing. Months may pass, the government said, before people would get their checks.

Futility.

He took a few deep, concentrated breaths, left the business strip, and continued on into the nearby residential neighborhood.

A woman held a trowel. A man pushed a lawnmower. Another jabbed at the earth with a shovel. Their movements were out of sync, something amiss in their rhythms, as if they were unconvinced of the meaning of their actions.

Three cars drove by in a caravan, celebrating a child's birthday, honking their horns and playing music, ribbons tied to their luggage racks and fenders, the kid in the backseat, looking out the window in disbelief that her birthday had come down to this. Neighbors waved in slow motion, like the people in the opening sequence from David Lynch's *Blue Velvet*, hypnotized, enacting half-hearted gestures of normalcy.

As he descended down to the lake, there were fewer people in their yards, and he thought of the long hours of lockdown ahead on a still-cold springtime Saturday. He passed by the house he and his family had lived in for twenty-one years, before they moved. He savored the permanent territory it occupied in the vault of his memories but, truth be told, he was never sentimental about the house after they sold it. They'd transported the texture of the place—its fluid auras of lived-in spaces, the warm tropical colors, the low accent lighting, the folk-art figurines and throw pillows—to their townhome when they'd moved, and the unfussy habits they'd cultivated over the years came with them. He enjoyed their new home's minimal maintenance requirements, all the outlets and fans and showers and drains in working order, the parking convenient and plentiful. Their HOA fees paid for the cleaning of gutters and dryer vents, the weeding and trimming and leaf blowing in the public spaces, a new paint job every decade. Beth had her office on the third floor overlooking the park. He had his studio. In fewer than ten years the value of their new house had more than doubled. They'd built a sizeable equity. Contributed to a SEP/IRA. Cut the cable-TV cord. Cancelled their home alarm system. Replaced expensive hotel stays with car camping. Bought health insurance under the Affordable Care Act and even managed to pay off their credit cards. They had so much equity in the house they opened a line of credit to use when they needed to make small remodels or buy a new car. Except—*except*—they carried a twenty-thousand-dollar balance on that line of credit and their health plan had a sky-high deductible and they only had enough in savings to cover their bills for one month and their checking account was so anemic it was in a kind of hospice.

At their age, a heart attack or cancer or a clumsy accident could be right around the corner. For that reason, Richard always took extra care stepping off curbs, never looked at his phone when crossing the street, drove the speed limit, and avoided adrenaline-junkie activities like paragliding and cave diving. Even with their tenuous finances he knew they were in better shape than a lot of other people, but their tidy little white-privileged existence was still threatened. In fact, he saw clearly—his feelings of futility building to something more like suffocation—that *everybody's* existence was threatened, even that of the filthy rich (their hobbyist spaceships could only manage liftoffs and landings, not escape). Homo Sapiens—the species itself—was on notice.

He returned home, anxiety somersaulting in his stomach.

That night, he awoke to the sound of coyotes. A chorus of yaps and yips. Acid rushed into his gut. He threw off the covers, took a short involuntary breath, looked at Beth asleep, caught the green smear of the digital clock on her side of the bed, and waited for it to come into focus.

Three a.m.

He listened. There it was again, an otherworldly staccato, riven up from a cleft in the urban veldt, as if the animals were gathering to take back the land humans had pushed them from, their yowls heralding a reclamation they believed was long overdue. He heard the death rattle of the yellow tape. A chill ran across his shoulders. *Cuidado.*

7

SACRIFICE

Flashing lights caromed like rocket glare off the dark windows of the townhomes and apartments. People took a break from washing the dinner dishes and came out of their homes. They stood apart in family groups, watching as seven fire trucks drove into their neighborhood, as the firefighters placed a ladder against an exterior wall of one of the public housing units. Smoke billowed from a second-floor window. *Billow.* The word only ever applies to smoke coming out of a building or car. Richard wasn't sure if what he saw could be described as billowing.

"See the smoke billowing out of the window?" he said to Beth.

Four of the firefighters went inside the front door.

"That's a lot of trucks for such a small fire," Beth said. "I'm not sure I see the smoke."

"Well, it's not really billowing anymore, I guess." He was reminded of the fire near the end of Tarkovsky's *The Sacrifice,* which he'd watched a few mornings before, in which an entire house was set ablaze, a black cloud flooding the sky.

With offices and bars and restaurants all closed, everyone seemed to be home in the neighborhood. Front doors open, people standing in their entryways, on sidewalks, talking in low conversations six feet apart, looking at the bright red trucks. Somali women and children gathered outside the smoky unit, their fathers nowhere to be seen.

The patriarchs of these large clans spent all day at their businesses. Buildings rented in the low-slung strip malls in the Rainier Valley. Grocery stores, espresso cafés, travel agencies, warehouses. They packaged discount flights to Mogadishu and sold burlap-wrapped kitchenware and rice bagged in jute. They managed taxi services and informal pools of Uber drivers. They fathered platoons of kids and then disappeared into worlds of international commerce, the trading of timeless goods. Richard had seen a few of these dads in the last couple of weeks, taking their younger children for walks, a rare sight. Their older sons, a group of kids who roamed the streets while their sisters were consigned to the household chores, were suddenly nowhere to be found in the daylight hours. With schools closed, perhaps these teens had been enlisted into their fathers' businesses. Sorting boxes of tea among aluminum shelving. Sweeping the floors of auto-body shops, sprinkling sawdust on oil drips. A few of the teens happened to be in the park, glancing over at the fire trucks, shrugging at each other, eager to get back to shooting hoops, an illicit game, given the restrictions on gathering in parks.

The firefighters huddled in their jackets, blocky figures in Kevlar and Nomex. Essential workers, along with police, EMTs, doctors, nurses, postal workers, delivery drivers, migrants who picked the country's fruit and vegetables, and the grocery-store clerks who stood behind plexiglass to ring up purchases. The uniformed, the minimum-waged, the undocumented, and the perennially exploited, these were the only people keeping the country running.

The flashing lights ricocheted against the light poles and garbage cans, the crosswalk signs and the large windows of the community center. Richard was transfixed by the generic nature of the emergency. For a few minutes, his broodiness, his funk, was on pause.

Eventually, people retreated into their houses and closed their doors. The boys resumed playing. The fire trucks peeled off one by one. The next day the online neighborhood chat forum reported that it was a dryer fire. Several bulging Hefty bags were now on the family's front porch, along with singed pieces of clothing stacked near their contorted mass of children's bicycles.

In *The Sacrifice,* Erland Josephson plays a narcissistic intellectual living in a comfortable home on a jut near the sea when an off-screen nuclear event forces him and his petulant family to become reluctant prisoners in the house. The intellectual declares himself to be an atheist, but he makes a plea to God that he will sacrifice his existence if everything can be turned back to the way it was. That night he is seduced by a witch, they levitate during sex, and when he awakens the next day the world is restored. Was it God or the witch who came through for him? Keeping his promise, he goes mad, burns down his house, and is hauled away by men in white coats. Ponderous, patience-testing, magnificent to contemplate and beautiful to gaze at —vintage Tarkovsky—the movie asks how much any one person is willing to give up in order to right the world.

Was Richard capable of such a sacrifice? Could he think of his despair as worth giving up for something outside himself? A connection, a comity, with others? Perhaps a small act, an offer to take the burned-out family's Hefty bags to the dump, would restore that connection. His cocoon of gloom was becoming too comfortable. It gave him license to disengage, to write the manifesto to his melancholy, to . . . whatever, but if left unchecked he could see how his panicky bursts of worthlessness could transmute into concrete visions of suicide, where you start to think of owning a gun as a good thing. It was now too easy to see nothing but scenes of doom everywhere he went, layering around his days like a fugue:

—The boarded-up windows of the Iglesia La Luz del Mundo. On the Sunday mornings before the pandemic, returning from his walks, he would cross the street outside the church along with families dressed in their Sunday best. The men in black suits and shiny black cowboy boots, the women in pink skirts with flowers in their hair. Little boys in sharp ties and gelled-back hair. Little girls in pleated chiffon. Holding their parents' hands as they strolled in for services. The church, recently remodeled and painted an ebullient robin's-egg blue, was now vacant and piling up unpaid bills. The sight of it almost brought him to tears.

—Two American bald eagles lying next to each other on the shoulder of the road. They were alive, one of the eagles squeaking in a strained, off-key bleat. Richard watched them from twenty yards away. How did they end up here? Their forlorn cheeping seemed unmatched by their grandeur, their fearsome wingspans and hooked beaks, which called for something more regal, in the category of growls or roars. Here was America's mascot, injured or despondent or both, brought low by the gravity of the existential crisis; a tilt of Earth's axis and the birds plummeted to the pavement, waiting for their avian intelligence to readjust to the unbalanced world.

—An ICU nurse on TV described the number of patients she was attending to on her shift: Eight patients connected to ventilators. Two intubated. Six expected to die that night, alone, their families saying goodbye over their cell phones. The nurse was talking via FaceTime from the front seat of her car in a dark parking lot, rain streaking down the back window, smearing the distant lights of the hospital into dim yellow swatches. She was taking a break, after having been on duty for thirteen embattled hours, her car like a foxhole in a war she was losing.

—In the lower latitudes of their neighborhood zip code, he rode his bike past the houses with cheap siding, the yards with brown grass and patches of dirt scuffed into circles by Dobermans, pickup trucks encased in blackberry vines. He pedaled along a street that had been closed to traffic so people could stroll and children could play. But on this beautiful late morning, filled with a radiating warmth, the streets were empty, the doors shut, voices absent, and—there it was again—*something*, a charge in the air, voltaic, a phantom lurking in the dead-end alleys.

—A cocktail hour on Zoom, an opportunity for a communal airing of grievances with four of their friends. David and Dolores, who lived only a couple of miles away, and Mitchell and Eve, now living part of the year in Arizona. They all missed Dolores' cooking, dinners consisting of grilled meats and finely singed asparagus, paradisiacal sauces, airy crisps constructed from parmesan cheese. He listened half-heartedly to the conversation, continually distracted by his mountain-man hair and the super-spreader event that was his stomach. Did he look woebegone? Hangdog? Long-faced? His friends liked him for his sardonic asides. They saw him as an extrovert; if not completely carefree, then untroubled. They would be surprised to know about the darkness seeping into his days. Mitchell and Eve said they had driven out to a remote area of the southern border where construction had resumed on the president's wall. They described bulldozers as large as dinosaurs, colossal dump trucks, gaping chasms in the earth, wide new dirt roads chewed up by industrial-grade tires, all of it happening out of sight of TV cameras. Another lie the president had told his followers—*Mexico will pay for the wall*—another lie they cheered, embraced, printed on coffee mugs and T-shirts, as if celebrating the brazenness of the lie and not the fulfillment of the promise was the whole point. Richard drifted away from the conversation, his eyes glazing over. Talk of the president created an odd friction in his thinking. He wanted him to fail—utterly and continuously—and he also wanted the pandemic to end, but he wanted it to end without the president reaping any electoral benefit from it ending, so perhaps it was best if the pandemic continued, at least through Election Day, killing as many people as necessary to seal the president's fate. Richard thought of it as similar to throwing virgins into a volcano. The Zoom conversation ended with the usual rundown of what people were watching on Netflix.

—A TV commercial touting a smartphone app called Houseparty, a "face to face social network," offering a way to "spend time with people you care about," where "being together is as easy as showing up," featuring built-in games such as Heads Up!, Quick Draw, and Chips and Guac, with several young people in market-researched skin tones separated into tiny boxes on the smartphone screen, having the time of their lives. He watched as he lifted weights, trying to tease out some definition in his biceps. The commercial depressed him on a molecular level. He could hear his DNA emitting tiny anguished screeches. He wanted to disengage from humanity. He wanted to be a cat or a stinkbug. He wanted to live out his days in solitude in a lighthouse on a storm-tossed coast, watching Turkish miserabilism on Blu-ray until his flesh merged with the upholstery of a comfortable chair.

—John Prine's death. After contracting the virus weeks earlier, the folk singer—his health compromised by a disfiguring cancer years before—had made a hard-fought climb back to stability, only to suddenly take a downward turn. Richard searched through his iTunes playlists for his favorite Prine songs: "Paradise," sung around campfires, which described the coal mining town where Prine grew up, the smell of snakes hanging in the air; "Angel From Montgomery," detailing the ache of living with someone who would come home from work every day with nothing to say; "Sam Stone," about the Vietnam War veteran whose heroin addiction destroyed the man's family, shooting all of their money into the hole in his arm; "My Mexican Home," a song about the special joy of escape, a man sitting on the porch in the tropical evening, bare feet on the cool tile of a patio, watching as the headlights of distant traffic traced across his kitchen wall. It was like John Prine himself had simply faded away.

Hard Times in Babylon

. . .

—The barren core of downtown, Richard walking through it looking for signs of life. He hoped to see lines of people waiting to buy their coffees and gourmet donuts, masked commuters surfacing from the underground light rail stations, cyclists rolling off the island ferries, office workers entering lobbies and making a break for the elevators, the klatch of drug dealers at the corner of Third and Pine, the homeless leaning like discarded lumber against the windows of the Gospel Mission, the tourists buying Bigfoot T-shirts at the Pike Place Market, the electric busses purring on Third Avenue. He walked first across the José Rizal bridge, named for the Filipino ophthalmologist and revolutionary hero of the Filipino people, executed by the Spanish colonial government when he was thirty-five years old. Looking over the side of the bridge Richard could see blue and gray and brown rain tarps speckling the sloping hill, piles of garbage marking the contours of a makeshift trail, and men wearing too many coats smoking near overturned grocery carts. In Chinatown, metal grates were pulled across restaurants and locked with heavy duty chains. Behind the doors, men and women may have been stacking crates of Hoisin sauce and boxes of ramen, their orders reduced due to the closed restaurants. The small park, the one with the paifang, a traditional Chinese arch, and the gathering place for the neighborhood's pigeons, was empty of people and of pigeons. He passed Post Alley near First Avenue and saw several tents erupting out of the sidewalks. On a pedestrian overpass there were more tents, congealed into a mass at one end of the walkway, some covered in shredded plastic, others with ripped windows and broken-zippered doorways. It was the type of vigorous Northwest morning that caused tourists visiting the city to marvel at its natural beauty and to crowd its market and to ride its giant waterfront Ferris wheel and to ascend to the top of its venerable Space Needle—but all Richard could think of was how forlorn it all seemed, as if the city would soon be closed for good. He walked up to Second Avenue. He saw workers in hardhats and green safety vests at the construction sites, with the usual concrete rubble and rebar at the ground level, and naked steel beams arising from the dust like the exoskeletons of alien life forms. He supposed these projects had been funded and begun before the pandemic hit, and the workers would continue to be paid, but who would inhabit or visit these buildings after they were finished? He continued up to Fourth Avenue, where the city's main public library consumed an entire block. The library had been designed by a world-renowned Dutch architect sixteen years ago, but the structure was cold and inscrutable, as if an ice tray had been crossbred with a Rubik's cube. The library's design and layout—and by extension its architect—held a deep contempt for human beings. The low ceilings and narrow escalators and tiny elevators and confused maze-like geography did not invite wandering. The fluorescent lighting managed somehow to be dim and harsh at the same time, discouraging to the practice of actual reading. The study rooms and children's spaces were made up of oddly constricting corners and vanishing hallways. And the main auditorium was a simple concrete shell that offered all the charm of a holding pen in a detention center. Richard could never pass by the place without reviewing all the reasons he hated it. The library was not an altar to literature and learning, but another plum in the tree of the architect's ego. The money spent on the eyesore could have fed the city's homeless for years. With the library now shut down, with no one entering and exiting, without the reflections of passing traffic in its glass windows, the few poor souls leaning against the exterior made the outlandish structure look like a relic from an abandoned futuristic city.

—Their pandemic relief checks arrived in the mail—$600 each and signed with the malignancy's name—and the next day they were quickly swallowed by a gluttonous maw of bills. The day after that Beth's unemployment claim of $4300 materialized in their bank account and they used the money to pay their taxes. These handouts they accepted without shame. They were a reimbursement of funds the president and his emetic spawn had grafted from the U.S. Treasury to pay for their gilded lifestyle: travel to and from the president's garish residence in Florida. His daughter's handbags. His repellant sons' business trips to desert sultanates and their wives' souvenir abayas. The First Lady's eyebrow plucks.

This was the music of Richard's disconsolate days, playing on a loop.

Taurus 9mm. Sig Sauer Luger. Canik TP9FSX. Mossberg 37251. Springfield Armory. Walther. Smith & Wesson, with ported fiber optics. Out of stock. Every single one. But he added them anyway to a shopping cart on Guns R Us, like it was a Blu-ray sale at Barnes & Noble. Just for research, he told himself. He planned to study the cost and dynamics of each weapon and remove them from the cart one by one, until he climbed out of his doldrums or until he clicked *buy*, whichever came first.

Could he put the barrel in his mouth? He knew of a man who lost his nerve just as he was pulling the trigger, pointing the gun ever so slightly to the left so that it blew off part of his cheek and ear. After surgery and rehab, the man actually didn't look so bad, but he still had to wake up every morning knowing he was the kind of person who couldn't even kill himself correctly.

Richard had trouble visualizing the act, in any form. Hanging seemed ghoulish. Pills could go wrong in a number of ways. Leaping off a bridge, forget it. Never would he choose to jump into a lake or a river, although that would be a sure bet, since he wasn't much of a swimmer. He thought of *Harold and Maude* and the absurd fake suicides Harold staged to get attention. Funny stuff.

How about throwing himself in front of a train? On his trip to France he'd almost been bashed by a bus. He was a half-second away from crossing a bus lane, looking right when he should have been looking left, confused by the arrow and the warning painted in big white French letters on the street. He was *that* close to stepping into the lane when something caught his ear, the tissue-like whoosh of a compression brake or a soft bell, and he looked left at the very moment the bus rushed past him, inches from his nose.

And then there was the time he was backpacking with his kids on a high and narrow ridge in the Olympics. They were all tired, looking forward to their camp for the night a mile away, when he tripped on a rock and fell face first on the trail. In slow motion, it seemed like then, the weight of his pack pulled him over the lip of the path. He began to tumble, picking up speed down the ridge face. He hadn't noticed the steepness and depth of the ravine until he was turning over for the third time. Suddenly he understood that if he didn't arrest his fall right away he would tumble all the way down to his death. He heard Chloe above yelling, "Dad! Stop!" This jolted him. He immediately threw out his legs and arms, his hands still clutching his trekking poles, stiffening against the rocks and heather, stopping his careening body only a few feet from the end of the brush, the last thing he could grab ahold of. He lay on his back, frozen in place, afraid any movement would be fatal. Below him loomed a thousand feet or more of jagged talus.

He caught his breath. Nothing seemed broken. The pack probably saved him from a back injury. He began to crawl ever so slowly on his hands and knees up to the trail, using his elbows to push himself to safety. There were bloody scrapes on his shoulder, his shin and calf and thigh, a swollen ridge above his left eye, a grated cheek, the blood already hardening into prickly little dots.

That night at camp, he rinsed off the dried blood in a mountain lake. Chloe broke out a flask of whiskey and they toasted to his survival. Once in his tent, he had trouble falling asleep, replaying the stumble and the somersaults, frightening himself with the thought of his children having almost seen their father torn to bits as he cartwheeled down the mountain.

Maybe he was living on borrowed time. Two near-death experiences in two years. He thought of the *Final Destination* movies that he watched with Zach, always the same storyline: someone in a group of polished young people has a premonition about a soon-to-occur disaster, a multicar pileup or a plane crash, and she convinces her group to flee before the disaster strikes. But then, in gory scene after gory scene, each member of the surviving group dies in a hideous accident. They cheated death, so death comes to claim them.

He'd been so careful since those two incidents, always hugging the inside part of the trail when hiking along a drop-off, always looking both ways before crossing the light rail tracks. So how did he expect to pull off suicide, gun or rope or pill or leap, when he was afraid of twisting his ankle on a curb?

And then, one evening, deep into his private gloom, he heard that Lina had OD'd, her body discovered in a bathroom of the house where she was staying in one of those run-down parts of Tacoma. The medical examiner called her father, who confirmed Lina's birth date and full name from her expired driver's license, described the tattoo of the butterfly on Lina's shoulder blade to the examiner, who replied, "Yes, that's what I'm looking at," and said he was sorry to deliver such awful news. That was it, the end, after twenty-five years, of Lina's life, and of the long-running anguished vigil of her father.

When Lina was fifteen she'd job-shadowed Richard as part of a school assignment. They drove around the city, shooting video for a few assorted clients, talking about photography, a skill in which the kid had shown some promise. He didn't know it then, but opioids were already likely turning her attention to their own grueling demands, settling into her bloodstream, filching her future. Her life had become a shadow of the girl she'd once been.

Her dad couldn't bear to see his daughter dead, so Richard offered to view the body if the coroner needed an eyewitness confirmation. Dead people were nothing new to him. During his time as a TV-news cameraman, he'd filmed the corpse of a cowboy face-down in a drainage canal in Colorado Springs, a woman lying dead half out of her car minutes after a traffic accident in Reno, naked bodies with tags on their toes in a Los Angeles morgue. He was in the rooms when his father and then his mother died, and he saw his brother's body, dead at nine from a congenital hole in his heart.

Only seven years old himself, Richard had accompanied his shattered parents to the funeral home to pick out a casket. They asked to see their son's body, now embalmed and clothed, and laid out on a gurney in a back room. Richard stared down at his brother, who he hadn't seen much of lately, in and out of hospitals for the last year. He reached down with his index finger and pressed hard on his dead brother's forehead, as if his body was something he'd found washed up on a beach, a starfish or a strand of kelp. He was shocked at how cold the skin was. He drew in a frightened breath and quickly pulled his finger back just as his mother grabbed his hand, saying "Don't do that!" He'd never forgotten the eerie waxy chill of the skin, *the temperature of death*, he told himself when he was older, when he could put words to the sensation.

Perhaps now, he thought selfishly, if he saw Lina's dead body he would be appalled and repelled by the specific finality of death, and this would scare him straight, bring him to his senses. But, as it turned out, it wasn't necessary to view the body. After the coroner signed off on the legal procedures and after an autopsy was conducted—standard in drug-overdose deaths—Lina was cremated. Now, what? Funeral? Memorial? No one knew exactly how to grieve. How to gather without gathering.

8

VOUCHER

Pulverized forests, sandblasted fields, the far-off drumbeat of explosions from a belching Earth. Starvation and cannibalism and the eating of insects. Dirty rain leaking out of a fistula sky. This was the future as depicted in John Hillcoat's adaptation of Cormac McCarthy's *The Road*. Richard saw it in a theater when it first came out and was so entranced he convinced Beth and Zach to go with him the next day to see it again. The movie depicted existence at the most desperate level of survival. An emaciated and dying father tries to keep his son alive in this unforgiving blight, wracked by the knowledge that he will soon be gone, leaving his boy alone in a pitiless world. But unlike Quinn's character in Fellini's very different road movie, the boy is rescued from his solitude by a wandering family offering a sliver of hope that the planet may be made livable again. Watching the movie for the tenth time in his studio, Richard was forced to consider the terms of his family's continued survival, and his own. As usual with the films he revisited over and over again, they always delivered up fresh secrets, new angles he had not previously considered.

He went upstairs, pulled down his empty backpack hanging in the laundry room, and began to stuff it with their two-person tent, his sleeping bag and pad, fuel canisters and a cookstove. He filled a cooler of water, resolving to dump it every two weeks and refill it with fresh water. He also considered filling their bathtub, like he'd seen in the movie, in case all the pipes stopped working. He wanted to double-check where he'd put his Swiss army knife and his headlamp. Beth still needed to restock the first aid kit.

Resolve. That's what he was feeling. A resolve to live rather than give up. When he sat down to check his email, he decided to delete all of his bookmarks for gun stores and clear his calendar of any reference to the gun range. But first—he couldn't help it—he clicked on the hours of operation for the range. It was still closed, but they'd updated their status. They were taking reservations for socially distanced gun safety classes beginning next week. He made a note of this on his calendar. What could it hurt, right?

He glanced at the headlines of his favorite news sites. *The New York Times,* the *Washington Post,* the *Guardian.* The United States had reached two milestones: one million cases of infections and 60,000 dead, more Americans than had died in the Vietnam War. On this momentous day in history, the president declared that his handling of the pandemic was "a great success" and his team produced a hastily edited video designed to tout his accomplishments.

As the video played, Richard watched the president gesturing towards the screen, nodding approvingly at the scroll of text and statistics and dates, as if he was presenting incontrovertible evidence of his mastery of the crisis. It made no difference to him that everyone in the room could see the video was nothing more than a piece of shoddy propaganda, that every fact was presented out of context, that every time stamp was misleading, that the quotes were cherry-picked and laid out in such a way as to destabilize the true chronology. It was a cheap piece of carnival hypnotism and the president was the unsavory barker, pointing and gesturing to the video proudly as if he were exhibiting a two-headed goat or a bearded lady with three breasts. *Behold the mysteries!*

All of humanity seemed to be coming undone at the seams. Sure, there were untold acts of compassion and small moments of tenderness—the frontline nurses and doctors, the food drives, the 30-percent tips for the restaurant workers filling countless to-go orders—but there was also a surly rejection of logic, truth, and brotherly love, cruelty for cruelty's sake, for no other reason than the puny thrill of it. This gleeful nihilism was evident in small pockets throughout the world, but nowhere was it more visible than in America. The rancor seethed around the edges of every discussion and gathering and meeting and task.

Maybe, Richard thought, the virus actually was not deadly *enough*. It did not kill like Ebola. It did not dissolve the body's internal organs like E. coli. It was not absolutely fatal like the first years of HIV. It did not cause swelled pustules of oozing Black Death. If it were a more gruesome and dependable killer, if it laid waste to third graders and house pets, then perhaps the president's benighted disciples would be taking the contagion more seriously, and everyone would come together to defeat it. Instead, his followers protested at state capitols, grunting about their freedoms and constitutional rights, proudly claiming they would never wear masks, while they carried AR-15s and rocket launchers into government buildings. They referred to themselves as the guardians of the Real America, but when faced with a deadly pathogen, they could not even summon the courage to wear a simple scrap of fabric across their mouths and noses.

Richard walked for two and a half hours. Hiking up neighborhood staircases and down wooded paths into ravines. Trudging across baseball diamonds and basketball courts. He moved briskly along the Chief Sealth trail, the pylons looming above him like giant sentries. He imagined them bent and twisted and cracked, like a scene from *The Road*, toppled and littering the ridge, the electricity they once carried long evaporated, their utility, their very power, a tale told from ancient history.

. . .

That night, he conducted one last scroll through the metronome of news before he went to bed:

Twenty-two million unemployed.

Prison inmates testing positive for the virus in alarming numbers.

Outbreaks at meatpacking plants threatening the nation's supply of quarter-pounders and double cheeseburgers.

New information detailing how the virus mutilated the body's insides. Strokes. Kidney disease. Permanent lung damage.

Reports of toe rashes as early indicators of infection, something to do with the immune system response.

New consensus on ventilators: They could kill you. Patients assigned to ventilators, apparently, rarely recovered. Ventilators now meant death when in the early days of the pandemic ventilators meant life.

He stared at his computer, no longer scrolling or even reading the words. The retinal glow of the screen became an abstract of fonts, bold type, italics, and the high-res colors of ads for items he had absentmindedly searched for in the last few days—Peckinpah Blu-rays, running shoes, outdoor heaters—casting back at him like taunts. Several seconds passed before he slowly looked up from his laptop and saw his reflection in the window of his studio, his face lit from below by the blue gleam. He decided, or rather he *considered* deciding, that maybe, *just maybe*, reading bad news every thirty minutes all day long was taking a toll on his psyche and spirit and attention span. That perhaps he should take a break, give it a rest, ease off. Even the idea of this, he realized, uncluttered his mind, only a little, but this was the first freshet of clearheadedness he'd had in weeks. There was really no reason to continue this infatuation with his misery, when he got right down to it, especially since his misery was only a thumbnail of the cinemascope of worldwide misery. Should he try a different approach? He felt a bothersome inkling of the thing he'd always fought against, and he looked away from his reflection in embarrassment. Yep, there it was, that thing, the thing he never trusted, didn't believe in, scoffed at and mocked: Positive fucking thinking.

He shut down his computer, closed the lid, left his phone in his studio to avoid temptation, turned off the light, and went up to their bedroom, where Beth had fallen asleep over her book. He washed his face and flossed and brushed his teeth, and then removed his pajamas, which he'd been wearing since early afternoon. He executed a few deep knee bends, straightened his legs and touched his toes, and then swallowed a dose of L-Threonate, another name straight out of a nineties sci-fi flick, a precious mineral fought over by intergalactic pirates (maybe played by Arnold Schwarzenegger and a young Sharon Stone). Except L-Threonate wasn't precious at all, it was magnesium, a common element in the human body. In small doses, magnesium worked in consort with the REM cycles to quiet the brain, facilitating elaborate, cinematic dreams, featuring cameo appearances by long-lost friends, rococo locations, and Escher-like landscapes. This was the first pill he'd taken since the pandemic began, but he remembered that—when it worked and he slept for eight hours—he'd attack the next day with an energy possessed only by athletes and hedge-fund managers.

Beth stirred. He kissed her goodnight, turned on his side, and stared at the streetlight peeking through the blinds. He recalled the one bit of uplifting news he'd read before closing his laptop. In the Indian state of Punjab, a generation of people had stopped in their tracks and stared in wonder at a section of the Himalayas that they'd never witnessed before, simply because it had always been obscured by smog. Before drifting off, Richard wondered if there were other new beauties to be seen in the world and if so, maybe, *maybe*, they were worth sticking around for.

Words began to dart like goldfish through his brain: triage, comorbidity, toe rash, shiv, ventilator, gun range, rocket, guacamole, cannibal, launcher, Punjab.

The next morning, he and Beth said goodbye to Chloe, who'd decided to move in with her boyfriend on his mountain property.

Richard felt the emptiness he always felt whenever their children left the house after a lengthy stay.

Beth went back upstairs to work and he went to his desk. He clicked on the gun range site and, before he could change his mind, made an appointment for a three-hour gun safety class. He told Beth it was a birthday present to himself and he invited her and Zach along, knowing his son had always wanted to fire a gun. She said no, she wasn't ready for that. Ready for what, no one really knew. The gun range website said they would first practice with a dummy gun, before moving on to the real thing and live ammo.

Beth's journal.
April 30:
It's 2:30am and I'm on the chaise in my office and I've been awake for more than an hour.

8:13 am. The numbers: 3.1 million cases worldwide; 227,675 dead. 1,045,300 cases in the U.S.; 60,945 dead. New York—305,024 cases; 23, 317 dead.

May 1:
Second Friday in Ramadan. The majestic tall man in black robe and purple-blue cap and white mask-scarf is strolling the park. Several paces behind, a small Asian lady in a fishing hat. Honking dad outside the corner house.

Blessed, blessed sleep.

Boy, was I wrong about the majestic man. He is wearing a big wooden cross.

May 4:
So much tragedy, world-wide.

May 10:
Happy Pandemic Mother's Day! I could imagine jumping in the lake. Must read up on safety re the virus. Water is still cold.

In the U.S., the number of dead tripling in 10 days!

. . .

On Mother's Day, Richard and Beth walked together along the lake. Usually, she walked while talking to her sisters on the phone or listening to the pastor from her church, who was now recording sermons on his laptop camera and uploading them to YouTube. Sometimes, she mixed her walks with running. Like his, her runs had slowed over the years, but she did a better job of keeping the weight off. She was more practiced than him at portion control and usually skipped the evening beer.

Mt. Rainier's eastern flank was visible to the south.

"I can't concentrate on anything," Beth said. "I feel like nothing I do matters. I mean, why bother?"

Her search for a publisher for her latest book had stalled out. She was frustrated by editors and agents, by the queries never answered and the submissions ignored. The rejections knocked her to the dirt and hammered away at her self-esteem. Richard's response to rejection was to let his mood sour to a fine rancor and then to email terse retorts to the funder or festival that blew him off, which left him with the sugar high of a burned bridge.

They stopped to hug. He could see she'd been crying before their walk. They did a lot of this these days, buoying each other in shifts, as if sharing a single tank of air while surrounded by sharks. He figured it was perfectly acceptable during these times to admit to a kind of defeat or surrender, to lay down arms, to hibernate for a while, and then emerge later with a clearer perspective. Old rules did not apply.

It was a beautiful morning, like biting into a crisp apple, a day not suited to interior terrors. They turned north. Mt. Baker was in the distance, an ice cream cone erupting from the earth. To the west, a jet groaned towards its landing.

"Have you thought much about when we might ever fly again?" he said, trying to change the subject. "I mean, just think, a couple years ago we were seriously thinking of recreating our round-the-world trip. What if we'd been in some far-off place, Kathmandu or Bangkok, when the pandemic hit?"

That trip, thirty-three years ago now, was for them a kind of giving field, a continual harvest of memories they would retrieve at unexpected times, when something—a note of world music, a dialect, a news item from a foreign country—reminded them of a sari in Jaipur or a field of kangaroos in Alice Springs.

"Sometimes, I'm not so sure I even want to take that trip," he said. "I wonder if the world has been spoiled by smartphones and Instagram, travel reduced to bucket lists."

"I know what you mean," Beth said. "Everything overbuilt, everything crowded, maybe too much of it looking the same. Remember when we were in Jaisalmer and we saw all those guys carrying what looked like chandeliers on poles through the streets? We couldn't figure out what the heck they were doing."

"Yeah, and it turned out it was wedding season and we would see those lights later at all the outdoor parties."

"I wonder if that is still a thing. Or has it been replaced by something else."

"Like a chandelier app or something."

"Maybe we'd still stumble on moments like that. That's what makes travel worth it, stumbling on stuff."

"I want to hope so," he said, sensing the itch of his private gloom. "I get what you're feeling, but you're not thinking of doing anything rash, are you?"

"Oh no, it's not that bad. I mean, you and I both know we've been down this road before. Trends are against us, we have to remember that, and look for other ways to find meaning in our lives."

"Right, we can't rely on others to validate us, to define us."

"You're better at that than me. I always blame myself and you blame others."

"Yeah," he laughed. "Really healthy, right?"

"I think it's healthier than wallowing, like I do."

"Well," he said, looking down at the ground, "I can certainly wallow at times myself." They walked the rest of the way in silence, holding hands, until they reached their car.

On the way home they made a quick stop at the store for nuts and cheese for happy hour.

. . .

David and James came by again at five-thirty. They all sat in their backyard instead of the alley, the sun now hanging above the western tree line, reluctant to drop. They could hear children laughing while throwing a Frisbee in the park.

"Well, I found out I have a touch of prostate cancer," David said. "They caught it early, but I'll be going in for twenty-eight rounds of radiation starting in July. Nothing like the radiation for my head and neck cancer though, thank God."

He was in good spirits, as if this time his bout of cancer was something he could manage with little fuss, where his previous cancer was frightening, scarring. These were two men who had already survived one devastating plague in the 1980s, back when they were in their twenties, both of them losing untold friends and lovers to AIDS. Now life had brought them, both in their sixties, another scourge, when the gift of reaching that age is to not take anything too seriously, to be able to say no to unwanted demands, to simply be present, to engage, to care, or to do none of those things if they chose not to.

"Are you worried about all those trips to the hospital?" Richard asked.

"You should be fine," Beth said. "I had to go in to get a mole removed, and it seemed really safe."

David said he wasn't worried, his appointments would last only a few minutes, a quick zap and that was all. Richard was now only half-listening, distracted, knowing that in a few days he would hold a loaded gun in his hand.

The shooting range was housed in a long rectangular warehouse behind a chain-link fence and a stand of evergreens, its entrance tucked around a metal partition, as if it didn't want to be found. He and Zach presented IDs, were escorted to a classroom, and then handed a sheet of paper, the rules of Gun Ownership 101 printed in all caps:

ASSUME ALL GUNS ARE ALWAYS LOADED.
NEVER POINT A FIREARM AT ANYTHING YOU ARE NOT WILLING TO SHOOT OR DESTROY.
KEEP YOUR FINGER OFF THE TRIGGER UNTIL YOU ARE READY TO SHOOT.
BE AWARE OF YOUR TARGET AND WHAT IS AROUND AND BEYOND IT.

The instructor, Brett, wore black-rimmed glasses and a black mask. Former marine. Volunteered at a nonprofit for suicide prevention. This detail was either comforting or ironic, Richard wasn't sure. Brett did not display the gung-ho bravado of some kind of self-appointed patriot, all muscled up, chewing tobacco and spitting into a Dixie cup. He looked like a web designer or a bartender at a brewpub.

"Most of the people I've been signing up are taking the class for self-defense," Brett said.

An ominous sign? Perhaps more people were nervous about a pandemic-fueled, post-election breakdown of society than they were letting on. Were the clients taking gun lessons hedonistic liberals, concerned with protecting their wine closets against neo-Nazis? Or were they right-wing extremists, tuning up their skills to repel a wave of antifa marauders?

Brett passed out another sheet titled Handgun Anatomy, along with plastic guns that resembled a Glock 44. Glock. A screenplay-ready name.

The ideal pistol to start or enhance your shooting experience. The innovative design of the hybrid steel-polymer slide chambered in our first .22 caliber round provides a lightweight and low recoil functionality for optimal control.

. . .

Brett had them stand up and practice The Fundamentals of Marksmanship: Stance. Grip. Sight Alignment and Sight Picture (he said this is what we all use to call aiming).

They studied the diagrams of a revolver and a semi-automatic: trigger. Trigger guard. Rear sight. Front sight.

The weapon was reduced to the sum of its parts. A tool, elegantly designed. A perfect working thing.

"Now, I'll show you how to hold it," Brett said. "Lean slightly forward over the toes."

They leaned awkwardly forward.

"Stretch out the arms. Grasp the Glock with two hands. Snug the left hand into the right hand and wrap it around the grip. Close one eye. Look through the foreground and background sights at a target several yards away."

Richard couldn't get either of his eyes to align with either of the sights.

"Firing a gun is a very unnatural act. The human body was not designed to assume a shooting stance, holding a chunk of metal with two hands pointing straight out from an erect body."

Brett explained trigger control as if describing the techniques of self-pleasuring. It involved subtle degrees of sensitivity: Point the index finger straight ahead. Lay it against the soft ridges of the barrel just above the inviting curve of the trigger guard, where inside rested a thin membrane of steel, the trigger itself, aching to be touched, caressed, pressed, until it exploded in heat and light with a deafening bark. Release the trigger gently but only halfway, the finger resting on it before, yes, another caress and another squeeze, another release, and then another explosion.

Brett exchanged their fake Glocks for one real Glock and one revolver. He escorted them to the firing range, which resembled what they'd seen in the movies. Individual stalls. Flat overhead light. Mechanical contraptions designed to ferry the paper targets back and forth. He told them that a customer was never allowed to rent a gun and use the firing range without a partner. This was to prevent a person from simply renting a gun to kill themselves. Richard found this unsettling, but his proximity now to an actual weapon had the effect of steering his thoughts away from self-harm to self-protection.

The wall behind the targets was composed of large rubber pellets, guaranteed to absorb the bullets, except the bullets they would be firing did not have the heft to travel the distance from the stalls to the targets, so Brett had them stand at a table positioned halfway into the firing zone, which they had all to themselves.

"Eyes and ears," he said, pointing to the goggles and ear protection.

They fired thirty rounds each from the Glock. The bullets disappearing into the wall of rubber. The sound was ear-splitting. This was why gunshots, at close range, could induce the kind of panic and confusion that ended with innocent people getting killed. This was what happened to Breonna Taylor, murdered in her Louisville home after police rammed their way in unannounced, mistakenly believing drug deals were going down. A man living there, Taylor's boyfriend and a licensed gun owner, thinking they were about to be robbed or attacked, fired when the cops broke down their door. The cops fired back. Somewhere between ten and twenty rounds ricocheted wildly through the rooms of the house, striking Taylor multiple times.

Richard inserted his bullets into the cylinder of the revolver. One by one. It felt like a ritual. A type of finality. How could depositing bullets into a gun be a preparation for anything other than violence? He snapped his cylinder shut, and thought of the Russian roulette scenes in *The Deer Hunter*. He imagined Brett speaking in Vietnamese.

They labored to pull the trigger—actually, to *press* the trigger, since *pressing* was the key to controlled firing. The trigger had to be pressed to first pull the hammer away from the chamber and then allow the hammer to surge forward and ignite the powder to propel the bullet. These moments seemed to last until the end of time. Zach had to pause, take deep breaths, reset his stance and check his grip. Richard had to realign and re-picture his sight. Christ, he thought, how could I kill anyone, including myself, if I can't even pull the trigger?

He'd paid around fourteen dollars for a plastic box of one hundred bullets. They fired fifty total, periodically stopping to examine the penny-sized holes they made in their targets. If the target had been a real human head, they would have maybe nicked an ear or grazed a scalp, but mostly the bullets would have landed somewhere beyond the target, in a storefront window or in the chest of an innocent bystander.

The lesson hadn't solved his dilemma. Gun or no gun. Buying a weapon would be easy, but mastering it would be time-consuming and expensive. He'd forever be afraid of it going off in his hand before he was ready for it to go off in his hand. Even the knowledge that it was sitting on a high shelf somewhere in their bedroom closet, hidden next to his python boots under a pile of old sweaters, would cause him sleepless nights. He took the remaining bullets home and put them in his tool box. Later, he learned there was a nationwide run on ammo.

Chloe and Zach came over later that week to celebrate both Mother's Day and Richard's sixty-second birthday. They ate baked steelhead, roasted Yukon golds with garlic and rosemary, asparagus sautéed in olive oil and sprinkled with Trader Joes' everything-but-the-bagel seasoning, arugula and spinach salad. After they cleared their plates, they moved outside into the evening light and started a fire in the chiminea. They drank an affordable red. Handed out cards. Shared a joint.

He didn't have a problem smoking weed with their kids, now that it was legal. He always kept something mild on hand, marketed with Northwest-friendly names—*Klamath Kush, Obama, Purple Haze.* Many of their friends didn't smoke, which puzzled him. Legal, safe, accessible grass had been everyone's dream forty years ago. They'd all survived Mexican ragweed, seeds and stems, the paraquat years, *Just Say No,* and Thai stick that was so unpredictable it could leave you giddy or embalmed, staring at the Pong ball pinging back and forth on the TV screen. Many of their friends and family members had smoked pot in their late teens and twenties before the years of kids and steady jobs and homeownership. But now, it was as if the ready availability of weed spooked them. Personally, Richard loved walking into a cannabis store and describing exactly what he wanted: A light head buzz lasting two hours. No paranoia. Around 17 to 20 percent THC. One or two hits at most. Good for a dinner party or a Scorsese film (*Goodfellas,* not *Age of Innocence*).

The weed clerks all looked the same: tattoos on their arms and necks, colored fingernails, a piercing or two, probably with a business degree folded under their stash box in a drawer in the bedroom in the house they shared with three roommates. They'd produce a small jar of pale green buds from the display case, harvested from the fecund watershed of a Washington forest, on sale for thirty-five dollars.

"Don't you sometimes think that all of the acrimony in the country would dissolve if marijuana was legal everywhere?" Richard said as he placed another log on the fire. "If you could buy it with your bank card at the grocery store like cookies and ice cream? Maybe that's why the red states are always so pissed off at us. They envy our mellow."

He and Beth fell easily into a repartee with their kids. Oft-repeated lines from their favorite films, light teasing, serious talk, good listening. Chloe would bring them up to date on her longtime friends (they called themselves The Floozies, a label they wielded more like a band name rather than as a description of their behavior). Zach would make comments in one of his movie accents, Australian farmhand or Cockney skinhead or the beast from Jean Cocteau's *La Belle et la Bête*. Richard had once told a friend that in the event of a zombie apocalypse he would want to be teamed up with his family. None of them knew how to fire a Bushmaster or field dress an elk but, as he explained, "we know each other, we trust each other, we won't leave anyone behind."

He was aware that their children's lives had expanded far beyond his ken, had become their own. Friends, lovers, a life made of their choices, the demands placed upon them, the secrets they wove within the intimacy of their companions—this is what any parent wants for their children, to follow the lines on a map of their own making. He held their time together, their memories and their promise of a future, as a warrant, an entitlement. He wanted to always be there for them, to listen, to remember, to ask questions, to offer answers or praise or critical advice when called upon. When he envisioned his own death, he was most sad not about his leaving, but about what he would miss of the living his kids still had in store for themselves.

Beth wrote him a birthday wish on textured paper, the color of tin, the surface like sandpaper left for centuries in a windstorm.

Dear Richard,

Here's a wish: May this be your one-and-only Pandemic Birthday.

This letter is actually a voucher. For what, you may ask? For the world. For our future enjoyment of so many things: a fresh-poured beer, consumed in a bar. A wine-soaked meal at the Virginia Inn or in Paris. Or New Orleans. Or who knows where? A movie in a theater. A play. A concert. A walk through a market in Mexico. Dancing in a plaza on a hot night.

It's also a voucher for all the pleasures we can enjoy sooner: hiking, camping, doing a push-up in a mountain river.

And for all the pleasures we can enjoy now: each other. Family, Friends. Zach & Chloe. Good food. Our home, indoors and out. Books. Movies. Coffee. Our cat.

I love you. Thank you for being my lifelong life raft.

Wasn't it true that suicide sometimes happened on a moment's notice, right when you thought a person was feeling better, looking better, only to have some night howl of fury descend on them out of nowhere, making it obvious they'd been kidding themselves all along, so they decided on the spot to go ahead with the act before they talked themselves out of it?

He couldn't imagine what that would feel like. The thought terrified him. Maybe it was the weed, but he picked up on some primal vibration of fear that would not allow it to happen.

9

ATTENTION

Their new portable heat lamp was positioned to the right of his chair. It warmed his face and torso and hands as he sat on the back porch, his dead mother's handmade afghan across his knees. He sipped his coffee and watched the sky dawning to daylight.

He'd left three books on the side table from the day before. James Salter's *Light Years*, William Styron's *Darkness Visible*, and *Guns for Dummies*. He lifted up the stack and his fingers touched a fourth book, underneath *Dummies*. It was a thin anthology of poetry from their collection in the upstairs bookcase. He had no memory of pulling it from the shelf, carrying it outside, placing it in the stack. How did it get here? There was a bookmark in the anthology that he recognized as his favorite, with an Egyptian design and a tassel that Chloe had given to him when she was eleven. He'd always leave it in a book and then forget where he last set it down.

The marked page was the poem "Sometimes" by Mary Oliver, a poet he was comfortable with. Most poetry he found so abstruse it made him feel stupid rather than enlightened, like the Iranian poet he once filmed who said the poem he'd just read had taken him so long to write—three or four years—that many of the lines in the poem related to earlier lines he'd long deleted, which explained why Richard found the poem incoherent. Oliver's poetry seemed to be written for ordinary people, but those with a desire for contemplation. Her deceptively rich, crisp observations of the mesh of the natural and spiritual worlds were invitations to live life at the ground level.

He read "Sometimes," pausing now and then after certain phrases. He liked " melancholy leaves me breathless" and "the sweet, electric drowse of creation." And then: "Instructions for living a life: / *Pay attention. / Be astonished. / Tell about it.*"

He stopped, and read those lines again.

"Instructions for living a life: *Pay attention. Be astonished. Tell about it.*"

And again.

He looked up from the poem, raised his eyes above the treetops, already thick with spring leaves, and saw the white contrails of a jet salting the sky. The dream catchers he'd purchased in a market on Isla Holbox trembled from the branches of the Japanese maple, the jagged edges of the tree's russet leaves like torn paper. He picked up his water bottle—its metal exterior warmed by the electric lamp—and tipped it to his lips, gulping the ice-cold water within. It was like drinking from a glacier.

Pay attention. Be astonished. Tell about it.

Something clicked, like a digital feed buffering into focus, a radio dial tuning to a static-free channel.

He'd had it all wrong, all this time.

He'd been doing nothing but wallowing in his murk, while all around him, everywhere, every day, common miracles were happening. All he had to do was pay attention to them.

A new path appeared, a way forward: Immerse in the minute-to-minute fabric of the hours. Find a solace in the here and now. Extinguish the hunger for answers.

Richard suddenly felt an urgent need to rewind the weeks and start fresh. Had he already wasted too much time? What had he missed? The pandemic would last at least the rest of May, probably well into June, quite possibly into the deep summer of July and August. Maybe it would never end. *Pay attention.*

The couple next door was arguing again, the wife raging in a monologue. *You don't live here anymore! I don't want you hanging around! This isn't your house.* The husband tried to defend himself, but he spoke too softly for Richard to hear. The wife, her voice rising. *I want you to leave. Leave now!* The shouting ended. Minutes later the husband made frequent trips in and out of their garage, gathering clothing and boxes to place in the back of his truck.

Richard finished his coffee and went into the kitchen. Beth was making her breakfast. He described the argument next door, filling in the details, but instead of annoyance at their neighbors for breaking the calm of his morning ritual he felt only sympathy for the couple and their two kids.

"We've been there," Beth replied. She reheated her coffee in the microwave.

"Were you reading this outside yesterday?" he asked, holding up the poetry anthology.

"No. What is it?" He handed it to her. "No, I haven't read that lately. Why?"

"Oh, just wondering. I saw it under my stack of books on the table outside and I have absolutely no memory of pulling it off the shelf."

He poured granola into a bowl, sprinkled blueberries on top, a squirt of honey, bananas and milk.

Beth hugged his arm, looked in his eyes. "You okay?"

"Yeah, sorry. Just brooding about, you know, *everything*. That was a really nice birthday, with the kids, the fire. Your card was beautiful, like a poem."

She squeezed his arm and leaned closer. "Let's hope it comes true. Your one and only pandemic birthday. Next year, things will be different. We have to hope."

He hugged her, and sensed a window opening.

Russet leaves. Torn paper. He wrote down the words in his journal, a knock-off Moleskine that he kept near his desk and had neglected for too long. *Glacier*, he wrote.

He began to look at the world with fresh eyes, like a visitor from another planet, observing Earth in all of its baffling beauty. The first of the sun's rays created archipelagos of light and shadow on the clematis and the maidenhair and the green aluminum shafts of the downspouts.

Suddenly, he experienced something altogether new. The albatross of ambition—always there, always hovering over his creative life—was lifting away. Richard had lived too long with a need to be noticed for his work, a need that was never satisfied by the transitory moments of regional fame, the paltry rewards of a few complimentary emails. The larger stage, the top-tier film festival, the national critique, always eluded him. "We live in the attention of others," Salter wrote, in *Light Years*.

Now, nothing seemed to matter as much as he thought it always had. The minutes and hours of the days ahead stretched to a vanishing point, free of obligation, free of ambition.

He checked his online calendar. It was as barren as the Great Plains after the buffalo. A quick scroll through his email revealed only a deluge of political pleas for money. The pandemic had already discharged him from the demands of social gatherings and dinner parties and holiday obligations (Richard liked people, really, he did—but he mostly liked them in the abstract). But now, he resolved to seek out impromptu interactions, to ask questions of the grocery store checker, to thank the lady who delivered their mail, to wave at strangers.

On his way to check their mailbox he saw Abdul getting ready to scoot on his back under a Honda. There had been instances in the past where he'd be returning from a walk and see Abdul out working and suddenly swerve to take a different route or pull out his phone pretending to answer a text, distraction practiced as theater. But now he wanted to see him, eager to let him know he valued these talks, that they mattered to him.

"How are you? Everyone still safe and healthy?"

Abdul nodded grimly through his mask. "Yes, okay, but my niece, she died."

"Oh no. I'm sorry to hear that. Was it…?"

"The Covid. She died last week. I talked to her a few days before."

"I'm so sorry." Richard had been avoiding checking the charts and tables and graphs in the *Times*, an incriminating report card documenting the country's failure, the infections multiplying so rapidly the numbers became almost meaningless, the virus swallowing people at will, churning randomly through the unhealthy and the unlucky.

"How old was she?"

"Forty-three."

Abdul himself was only in his late fifties. He had diabetes and high blood pressure and sore joints. He'd started exercising. Walks and slow jogs. Richard saw him out with his wife, both of them jogging, Abdul in sweatpants and she in her hijab. He'd lost weight and said he was feeling better, but he didn't work on cars as much as he used to, and he was now on disability.

"Will there be a funeral?"

"She already buried. At the All-Muslim Cemetery, in Covington. We couldn't go in. We had to stay outside and watch them bury her through the fence. She was health worker. For people in their houses."

Abdul shook his head. He didn't seem to want to talk more.

"I'm so sorry," Richard repeated, now at a loss. He thought of saying something like "hang in there" but then realized that not only would he probably have to explain that phrase to Abdul but that it was a stupid thing to say in the first place.

Richard gave himself permission to stop jogging. The last time he'd attempted a three-mile run his legs were as heavy and stiff as fence posts, and the jogging only seemed to *add* another pound or two to his frame. How long might it take him before he reached the unexplored territory of morbid obesity, along the lines of, say, late-stage Orson Welles? He decided not to worry about it.

People everywhere were making pledges and resolutions, maybe because they finally had the time in their harried existence to slow down, take stock, reflect. Some pledged to lose twenty-five pounds, some pledged to give up carbs. Others pledged to give up drinking, conceive a child, start a new romance. Richard had stuck to his pledge to not cut his hair. It now splayed down the back of his neck like an aging roadie's, with flecks of gray sprouting directly from the scalp. But he didn't care about that either. The concessions to his appearance no longer mattered.

Now well into May, he received an email from the general manager at the radio station, announcing that deejays could start to produce their programs from home. The news thrilled him. In the weeks since programming was cancelled, the station, once known for its eclectic menu of world music, bluegrass, folk, alternative country, reggae, funk, and blues, had been playing an automated algorithmic clusterfuck of adult-oriented pop rock, without point of view or personality. Richard went to work immediately planning a theme show he called Songs for Sheltering in Place, writing down the titles that jumped out at him from his collection of music: Willie Nelson's "Hello Walls"; Warren Zevon's "Mohammed's Radio"; Eliza Gilkyson's "Hard Times in Babylon"; Bob Dylan's "Shelter From the Storm," as sung by Rodney Crowell and Emmylou Harris; and a road-weary version of Townes Van Zandt's "Lungs," a song that dwells on the insulin coma therapy that permanently rattled the singer's brain chemistry, before it shifts to a troubling magic realism about his bitter fight to breathe the life that's passing.

For Richard, the music was a kind of serum, an antidote, to the dark poison of the preoccupations that had been haunting him. He compiled his playlist, dragged the music files into folders, wrote a script, recorded the audio, and cut it all together in Final Cut Pro. The program was ready to go by the end of the week.

. . .

Richard wanted to surround himself with trees, he wrote, *to step in and out of shadows, to see sunlight flickering through leaves as if from an invisible projector. He wanted to bathe in the soothing Fahrenheits of a Pacific Northwest spring, the warmth soft as fur. He wanted to run his fingers through it.*

On a Sunday, he walked the three miles from his home to Seward Park, listening to old-school ska and rocksteady on his phone. Reggae had always lightened his moods. It was hard to dwell on the troubles in the world with the Wailing Souls' "Jah Give Us Life to Live" pulsing in his earbuds. He followed the route along Lake Washington. Goslings paddled single-file between their parents. An otter bobbed close to shore. A runner came towards him and they carved out an oval of grass between them for the few seconds they existed in the same air space.

The day before Richard had fulfilled a birthday wish: to finally watch the five-hour director's cut of a lost masterpiece, Bernardo Bertolucci's *1900*. Zach had downloaded it from the internet a few weeks earlier, using BitTorrent to corral the film's digital particles into his laptop. As he walked, Richard relived the film's images, the way that he and Beth and Zach simply surrendered to the entire day.

"I think it's been thirty years since I've seen this," Richard said to them as they retreated to his studio in mid-afternoon and closed the hardwood blinds to block out the sunlight. They silenced their phones, spoke only in whispers, the studio a place of witness.

They sank into Bertolucci's extravagant vision, painted on a cinematic canvas that spanned decades, with an international ensemble of actors—De Niro, Depardieu, Lancaster, Hayden, Sandrelli, Sanda, Sutherland—playing outsized characters in a revolving carousel of fascism, repression, rivalry, sex, and perversion. The viewing spanned seven hours, with breaks to make coffee and scavenge chocolate, to exchange critiques and register moments of wonder. When the afternoon dissolved to early evening, they drank glasses of beer and munched kettle chips as DeNiro and Depardieu aged on screen. They took another break to prepare dinner, pasta with red sauce, lamb sausage, onions and peppers. They opened wine. The film digitally unspooled its spell, transporting them back in time. The pandemic world was neutralized, pushed away as if on a raft, receding to a curved horizon and spilling off the edge of the planet.

He continued his walk, past the shuttered boathouse, the chained-off parking lot, the locked bathroom. He bounced to Gregory Isaacs' "Cool Down the Pace."

Women pushing strollers. Bikers and skaters. Older couples with bandannas hanging below their chins. Cherry blossoms littering the ground. In the east Richard saw a section of the Cascades he'd never noticed before, a mandible of jagged peaks far to the north, snow sprinkling their crowns. Children played on the north beach, lifting up handfuls of pebbles glinting in the sun like fool's gold. Algae quivered in the shallows at lake's edge. He wanted to lie on his back in the water and drink the heat of the day.

The lakefront path reached its terminus at Seward Park and then circled around the exterior of the park's old-growth forest. He walked for a bit along the sunny east side and then plunged into the woods, scaling the wooden staircase that delivered him to an Eden of swaying big-leaf maples and Douglas firs, horsetails and sword ferns, logs cloaked with moss, glens carpeted in twinflower, meadows of salal and Oregon grape.

Cavalries of horsetails. Quivers of sword ferns. Meadows of salal and Oregon grape.

All of it, he wrote all of it down.

A rectangle of sunlight was carved into the floor of a glade, the edges feathered into the outline of a cathedral. He walked into it and tilted his face to the sky, the sun imprinting circles under his eyelids.

. . .

The next morning, he awoke from a near eight-hour sleep with a renewed enthusiasm. He turned off NPR while he made the coffee, tired of the hourly repetition of the reporters' updates, delivered in their succinct, officious syntax. He switched his phone to airplane mode.

At his desk, with a piece of typing paper, a ruler, and a pen, he designed a simple columned sheet to replace the Post-its they used as a shopping list. He divided the list into sections according to the left-to-right sweep of the store's layout: PRODUCE. BULK ITEMS. FROZEN. DAIRY. DRY FOODS. MEAT AND FISH. BREAD. He printed out twenty copies and showed Beth his handiwork.

"So this is what you've been doing since you got up?"

"I felt like a kid in grade school," he said.

She examined the grid. "I like it!"

"A stroke of analog ingenuity, right?"

"Maybe you could market these on Etsy or somewhere," said Beth.

He shook his head. "Nope. I'm free of ambition, remember?"

They filled in one of the lists for their morning supply run. They used to walk or ride their bikes to the store in the summers, buying only enough food for dinner that night or breakfast the next day, whatever would fit in a knapsack. But now they bought enough food to fill three tote bags, provisions for at least a week.

The parking garage was still nearly empty at eight. They tore the list in half and split up, each with their own cart. Beth handled PRODUCE and DAIRY. Richard took on BULK, DRY, and MEAT. He was sometimes flummoxed by the differences in steel-cut oats, the varied textures of dry coconut, the flavors of boxed teas. Not wanting to linger in the store, he rushed and made mistakes. Malted milk balls instead of dark chocolate almonds. Skinless thighs instead of skinless breasts. He bought a frozen pizza—something they never ate —figuring they would be happy to have it when all of their other food had been consumed and Hell's hounds were growling at the gate.

They used to have bags of dried soup beans in their pantry. Little flower-print bags of beans tied with ribbons, a gift from Richard's mother that she bought for them at her community center's Christmas bazaar when she was still alive. Beth had told him to save them for the apocalypse, and he responded by saying, "That will never happen." One day he got tired of them cluttering up the shelf, so he chucked them in the garbage. Now, today, cursing himself for throwing them out, he bought twelve cans of soup. Chicken noodle and beef barley and vegetable medley and stacked them in the pantry where the little bags used to be.

Their new list reduced their time in the grocery store to no more than twenty minutes. They felt safe, even energized, by this crisp efficiency.

Up next: their drink. Some people considered their body a temple, but Richard thought of his as more like a flask. In the Before Times, he'd wander the aisles of a nearby wine shop, organized by regions—Columbia Plateau, Rhone Valley, Tuscany—and load up a cart with a dozen or so new labels every few weeks. Now, he ordered their wine and beer online from Total Wine, the nearest store located in a mall near the airport, a twenty-minute drive away. He found a few Zinfandels and Malbecs and PicPouls he liked, his favorite IPAs and Pale Ales and Porters, a fifth of Bulleit Rye. He backed into a designated parking spot, texted the store, opened up the trunk, and ten minutes later a kid in a mask—Richard's factotum, his vassal—strode out pushing an oxcart full of booze.

Next up, Costco.

The store occupied several football fields of land in the industrial flats of the city. Cars drove in and out of the parking lot like Holsteins returning to a trough. Everyone wore masks, brushing past each other in crowded aisles, clogging the lane that housed the holy grail of toilet paper, massing near the roasted chicken as though receiving communion. He tried to move briskly in a clockwise sweep, to replicate the deftness he'd mastered at their grocery store, but invariably Costco had stocked reliable items in new places within the layout. He was forced to retrace his route back and forth through the vast maze of the store, to search once again for the trawler of sun-dried tomatoes, the pallet of gluten-free crackers, the grove of satsumas. He got lost among the scaffolds of dried pasta and the bathtub-sized jars of peanut butter. Shoppers moved in swarms, urgent and furtive, their eyes peering from above their masks with a wolfish avidity, scanning the racks of olive oil and chocolate syrup and Country Time lemonade. They looked like creatures without mouths, a migration of larvae.

He spent $425 at Costco. $510 at Total Wine. $218 at the grocery store.

The promise of summer has turned into a tease. Beaches opened and then closed. Vacant sands and empty lifeguard chairs.
The stopped world.
But the heat will come, perhaps earlier this year than last. He wanted to savor these cool nights of the blossoming spring.

That evening, Beth went to work picking through a head of romaine, culling leaves that to him looked perfectly healthy but to her eyes were tainted with blight. She discarded edible matter with ruthless intensity, reducing a bushel big enough to feed the Brady Bunch to a salad for two. They ate their dinner—pan-fried trout in butter and lemon and garlic, roasted red potatoes, the salad—in the backyard on a folding table, under the Japanese maple now nearing full bloom. There was enough warmth in the evening air to require only a sweater and light wool socks, the electric outdoor heater on standby.

Richard may have removed himself from obligation, but the virus had not retreated in the least. It had not surrendered. Social distancing and mask-wearing appeared to be working in the nation's largest cities, with emergency field hospitals dismantled and refrigerated trucks sent back to the lot, but the virus had simply moved on to new targets wherever it could find them. Midsized southern cities—Louisville and Mobile and Nashville—experienced crowded emergency rooms and overstressed ICUs.

The pathogen was on track to notch one hundred thousand kills by the middle of the week.

10

UNRAVELING

Richard made their coffee and turkey sandwiches while Beth packed protein bars and oranges. They filled their water bottles and threw layers of extra clothes into their knapsacks. They drove up Interstate 90 towards the thicket of trails crisscrossing the western slope of the Cascades. It was the Tuesday after Memorial Day, and the governor had reopened some trails for day use only. They were determined to hike for the first time since the pandemic began.

Twenty years ago, they'd explored many of these paths with their children, rousing them out of bed on Saturday mornings, feeding them chocolate muffins, parking at trailheads and draining the last of their coffee before changing into hiking boots. But in the last decade, the trails had come to feel like ant tracks, overrun on weekends with packs of young workers from Amazon, dressed in expensive microfibers, discussing valuations and burn rates, accompanied by their dogs Terri and Bryan and Bobbi.

Seven a.m. A parking lot for a popular hike was already overstuffed with Outbacks and Foresters, but their trailhead was two miles further along, where the lot was still empty. They parked, quickly laced their boots, gathered up their trekking poles, bandannas, and spare masks, and ascended the trail. How were they going to manage the inevitable encounters with other hikers? Pull up their bandannas, turn their heads away, and pass without a word? Do they try to step off the trail into the surrounding vegetation? New studies showed that the virus did not leap from person to person like a flea and that it was much less likely to spread outdoors. It thrived best in enclosed spaces with poor air circulation. But what if others had not yet absorbed that news, or disputed it, or simply wanted to practice caution?

They passed through a chapel of old-growth fir, emerged into a long stretch of white-fleshed birch, and hopped over wet tendrils of snowmelt. Four and a half miles later, they arrived at a lake pooled at the base of a cirque. They submerged their feet in the frigid lake and luxuriated in this modest first flush of summer, the sun having dissolved what was left of the thin cloud cover. There was a whiff of skunkweed along the marshy contours of the lake. They ate their lunch.

He closed his eyes, listening to the lake trickle into a stream, heard the soft buzz of a bumblebee, and visualized a future United States where neighborhoods and regions are protected by drawbridges and checkpoints, walls and electrified fences. The people within, vaccinated against the virus, would live like the Indians of the Mato Grosso, self-governing and self-contained, wary of outsiders, their wardrobes stocked with animal skins and necklaces made from the toenails of marsupials. They would have their own privatized internet and sustainable food supply. Solar arrays on every house and every car, forests to roam through and lakes to splash in. A land of harmony, while outside the walls the president's disciples will live like cannibals on scorched, disease-ridden plains.

Other hikers arrived, breaking the skin of this fantasy. Small groups of young people mostly. Some solo. Richard and Beth put on their socks and boots and started the descent, raising their bandannas over their mouths and noses when necessary. The young hikers they passed on the way down were maskless, but they stood off the trail until he and Beth went by. Older hikers were also on their way up. They wore masks, and as an extra precaution they scampered into the brush and turned their heads away when Richard and Beth passed. This seemed a tad overdramatic. Nobody exchanged greetings or commented on the beautiful weather. Was the breezy fellowship of hiking another one of the pandemic's casualties?

"I read that they're saying the pandemic might be around for years," said Richard. "That it may never go away. It might settle into a flu-like pattern, not as lethal nor as contagious as it is now."

"Yeah, I heard that," said Beth, walking in front of him. "It might be like the common cold." Scientists were saying, in so many words, that the future of the virus depended on its hosts' future, on the degree of respect for it, on how often and under what circumstances the hosts fed its voracious appetite. If it turned out to be a virus with tenacity, possessed of a will to live, it would become less deadly, since it needed new hosts to supply it with regular portions of healthy cells. It would keep humans alive so it could feed off them.

They returned to a nearly full parking lot. They tossed their packs onto the backseat and exchanged their hiking boots for sandals and Crocs. Maybe a summer of hiking and camping, of living outdoors as much as they could, was possible after all.

Back home, after rinsing the mud off his hiking boots and hanging up his daypack, while he waited for his turn in the shower, Richard clicked on the video clip he'd heard about the day before. He had tried to resist watching it—after all, how much more ugliness could he stand—but the buzz around the video was both inescapable and depressing. Another Black man killed by the police. What else is new in America?

It was difficult, at first, while watching the video, to understand what he was seeing. Yes, he knew this Black man had died, and yes, it was plain to see a white policeman with his left knee pressing into the Black man's neck, but there was something almost conceptual about it, as if this is what it might *look like* for a white cop to slowly murder a Black man, but surely this wasn't what the cop was actually doing. Surely the white policeman could see the smartphones filming him and hear the bystanders calling out for him to stop. Surely he would quickly end this simulation of a murder and get off the man's neck.

The Black man was being held face down on the pavement. He kept repeating, "I can't breathe. I can't breathe." His hands were cuffed behind his back. Another police officer was leaning over the man, just out of the frame, and another officer was in the background, also partially out of the frame of action. There was a cop standing guard, his arms spread open, preventing any bystanders from coming closer. The bystanders were pleading to the cops to stop, to get off the man, to let him breathe. What had happened before the man wound up face down on the pavement with his hands cuffed behind him and a tall and muscular policeman kneeling on his neck? Had the man killed someone? Stabbed someone? Robbed someone at gunpoint? Richard had read something about a forgery, but why would passing a bad check or using a counterfeit bill lead to his death?

The white cop insisted on keeping his knee jammed in the man's neck and his left hand seemed to be clenched in a fist and jammed into his pocket as he pressed his left knee down, the fist adding a little extra pressure as the man's face was ground into the gritty surface of the pavement.

The man made a retching sound.

The unbroken video was like a film clip from a piece of slow cinema, the kind of films Richard admired for their rigorous adherence to the passing of real time, as if time were a character, with moods and agency. There were no edits. This is what it looked like to methodically crush the life out of a person. The bystanders were the off-screen extras. When one bystander made a move to rush to the tortured man's aid, the grinding killer cop suddenly drew his mace from a holster and aimed it at the bystander. The gesture was odd and startled, as if the white killer cop were suddenly agitated, concerned that he might be stopped before he completed his mission. The gesture ruptured the trance of real time and signaled a change in the arc of the video.

The bystanders noticed the blankness of the Black man's expression, an absence of tension in his prone body. Something had gone out of him. They called out for the cops to check his pulse. "He's not breathing," they said. "Check his pulse," they said. But the murdering white grinding cop kept his knee on the man's neck and his left fist in his pocket.

Eight or nine minutes later, an ambulance arrived.

The cop stood up and with the help of the other cops they dragged the man a foot or two on the pavement before turning him over. The Black man's head flopped like a dead man's head, like a victim in a snuff film. The ambulance crew picked him up to put him on the stretcher. Still no one had checked his pulse. No one was in any hurry. He was, after all, just another dead Black man.

His name was George Floyd.

Upstairs, Beth was dressed and brushing her hair at the sink. Richard came in, a little shell-shocked, and told her what he'd seen. She didn't want to watch it for herself, his description was enough, and when he thought he should watch it again to be sure of what had happened he realized this would diminish the shock, it might turn the grotesque into the clinical, and this would desensitize him to the horror.

That evening the demonstrations began.

Over the next several days, Richard and Beth watched the nightly news as if viewing raw documentary footage assembled into a rough cut. In Minneapolis, the city in which George Floyd lived and died, protestors marched and raised fists and kneeled deep into the night. The protests soon spread to other city streets. Chicago, Los Angeles, Atlanta, New York, Portland, Seattle. Among the protestors were some who came with backpacks full of rocks and frozen water bottles which they used to smash windows of department stores and restaurants. A few looted and started fires.

The police, heavily geared up in bulletproof vests and helmets, charged protestors in the night, clearing them away with pepper spray, tear gas, and flash-bang grenades. Wikipedia described these as "less-lethal explosive devices used to temporarily disorient an enemy's senses." The description was written in language intended for SWAT-team manuals and paramilitary pamphlets, the flash-bangs measured in candlepower and decibels. Victims of the blasts "perceive an afterimage which impairs their aim." The loud volume "causes temporary deafness" and also "disturbs the fluid in the ear, causing a loss of balance." The intensity of the explosions can "ignite flammable materials."

The streets looked like they were lit by a cinematographer. Bursts of white light and roiling smoke, burning police cars dotting the frame as if placed there by an art director. Sand-colored Humvees squatting in deep-focus *mise en scène*, the sulfured glow of their mounted lamps like the eyes of giant beasts. Helmeted robots were etched against a background of flames. Pepper-spray canisters were drawn from holsters and emptied into the faces of young people. There were panicked scrambles backwards and sideways over shattered glass and between parked cars. People were screaming.

These were scenes of purge. A purge of cooped-up anger and frustration. This was the chaos that some had predicted since the reality-TV star was elected four years ago. It somehow made sense that the murder of a Black man would be the flashpoint for the final unraveling.

The pandemic vanished from the twenty-four-hour TV news cycle. The daily reports of new cases and deaths, of infection rates and vaccine trials, were swept from the home screens and front pages by the protests and the violence. For several nights the George Floyd fury burned. In the mornings, downtowns were clotted with tension and surrounded by a vaporous haze.

After a searing night of broken windows and blazing fires and arrests, volunteers cleaned up the debris. The next night, more destruction.

Richard found it difficult to work up the appropriate sympathy for a vandalized department store. The cost of repairs and lost merchandise could be reimbursed directly from the expense accounts of the corporate CEOs of Nike and Starbucks and Target and then written off on their tax returns.

On the Monday morning a week after George Floyd was murdered, Richard and Beth drove downtown, parked, and wandered the central network of streets. He brought his video camera. Beth brought garbage bags, intending to aid in the clean-up. But the streets had already been cleaned, and they were all but deserted. A few restaurants were open, selling takeout, but most were closed and boarded up. Plywood covered department store window displays. Security guards leaned against locked doors, checking their phones. A paid crew of so-called ambassadors, homeless people employed by the chamber of commerce to regularly sweep up coffee lids and cigarette butts, were now painting over graffiti and impromptu murals, a rush to whitewash the unfolding history.

Richard filmed a mural of George Floyd painted on one of the plywood sheets. The head-and-shoulders, straight-to-camera portrait first appeared in a photograph of Floyd shortly after his murder. His expression is calm, relaxed, smiling ever so slightly. Within days, the photo had inspired murals in Kenya, Syria, the West Bank, London, and all over the United States.

The protests continued, night after night after night. Around the world people marched. Rome, Berlin, Paris. One day a seething crowd swarmed outside the fence of the White House and the president was hustled to an underground bunker. Later, he claimed that he was merely inspecting the structure. No one believed him. His cowardice was well documented. He had escaped the draft as a young man when a doctor faked a diagnosis of bone spurs. He walked away from his bankrupt businesses. He paid off the students hoodwinked by his phony university. His entire life was one of all-consuming gutlessness. Later, the attorney general admitted the president was shuttled off to the bunker as a security measure.

The president made a statement from the Rose Garden, a place he regularly befouled with totalitarian proclamations, and where he now stood flanked by his cartoonish junta: The crash test dummy, the massive henge of flesh that was his attorney general, the son-in-law who strode the White House grounds like an entitled duke, the duke's wife—the president's daughter—exuding the decorative bearing of plastic fruit, and the blonde-tressed press secretary in trophy-wife heels who lied to the press her first day on the job when she said, "I will never lie to you."

The president announced the deployment of troops to quell the unrest on American streets. Off-screen, the attorney general instructed the police and the National Guard to immediately disperse the peacefully assembled protestors in nearby Lafayette Square. The officers and the troops advanced into the square where the protestors were milling about.

Richard watched it all on his laptop screen, his eyes panning and tilting, zooming in on details, scribbling them down in his notebook: *Gas canisters launched into the crowd. Shields driven into the stomachs of people standing with their hands up. Chemical sprays shot into faces. Police on horseback swinging batons. Peaceful protestors dashing for cover, tripping, crumpling to the ground. A toxic fog enveloping the melee.*

Within minutes helicopters whirred overhead and cleared the haze. The president then lumbered into the scene, his gait slowed by his daily intake of processed meats, his spaniels trotting behind him. His daughter lifted a Bible from her designer purse and handed it to her father like she was a prop girl in a piece of shabby theater. He turned and faced the press, nodding for the cameras with a manufactured expression of steel-eyed grit—pretending he was overlooking a smoldering landscape of vanquished enemies—and gripped the Bible in one hand, then the other, weighing it, judging its volume, as if it were a cantaloupe. He held the cantaloupe near his head with his right hand. He re-fixed the steely expression, his eyes a phony squint, his skin an orange paste, his hair a flaxen tiramisu. He invited members of his bewildered junta to join him. They grouped around him in an awkward tableau, unsure of this moment's point or purpose.

The press, almost immediately, responded with predictable

disgust, with the recycled, exclamatory condemnation that "the president has reached rock bottom."

But wait, Richard wrote, *wait a minute. Hadn't the president reached rock bottom long before this? Maybe when he lied about those bone spurs? Or when he ignored the exoneration of five innocent boys wrongly convicted of a long-ago rape in Central Park? Or when he commissioned a portrait of himself and used charity donations to pay for it? Or when he bought off that porn star to keep her quiet during his presidential campaign? How many rock bottoms does he get?*

Richard believed the president had been rooting around the bottom for decades, wallowing in the muck of his mortifying self-regard while searching for the trapdoor on the bottom's floor. After spreading a contemptible lie about the former Black president's birthplace, a lie that helped get him elected to the country's highest office, he knew he'd finally discovered the handle to that door. After lifting it, revealing a shaft descending into a void, he gleefully plunged down the abyss in a free fall. Here, in this bottomless pit of extravagant vulgarity, the president understood he could do and say anything and get away with it.

A few days later thousands of people crowded into a park in Rainier Valley, two miles south of New Rainier Vista. They carried signs: Defund the Police. Black Lives Matter. Justice Mercy Peace Love. They marched through streets where Black lives often did not matter but where many Black people lived. Chloe and Zach were in the thick of the crowd in the middle of the street; Richard and Beth kept to the fringes. Residents came out on their lawns to watch and applaud and film with their smartphones. The demonstrators turned south on Rainier Avenue, the hazy outline of the mountain popping up behind Payday Loan and Discount Donut signs. Refugees looked on from the balconies of their public housing units. Immigrants filmed from behind their fences. Mexican-American and Asian-American business owners handed out water bottles and spurts of hand sanitizer.

People engaged in a call-and-response, shouting through their masks: Say his name! George Floyd! Say her name! Breonna Taylor!

For the first time since lockdown began, Richard felt the flush of kinship with other people, people as a force outside himself. He was attuned to every snap and vibration in the throng. He wondered how many others in the crowd were clawing their way out of despair or depression or self-pity? How many others now felt more alive during this deadly pandemic than they ever had before?

Volunteer bicyclists handled traffic control. They rerouted cars and formed cordons to guard against drivers crossing into the demonstrators' corridor. There was not a police officer in sight.

One young man, leading chants in the middle of the masked crowd, had pulled his mask below his chin, and the spit from his energized shouts was backlit by the afternoon sun.

"Let's keep moving," Beth said, grabbing Richard's arm and swerving them back to the periphery. They placed their trust in the masks, the outdoor air, the mid-70s temperatures, and the steady flow along the outside sidewalks to mitigate any opening sensed by the virus. The pathogen, undeterred, found other ways to keep at it.

An online graph in the *Times* depicted the number of positive cases and deaths since the virus arrived in late February. The graph, set in sharp blocks representing individual weeks, resembled the cityscape from the overture to *West Side Story*, a black outline of buildings against the sky, a veritable Manhattan of infections. One hundred and ten thousand dead in America. The most in any nation anywhere on the globe.

11

ESCAPE

Daylight clung to the evening sky like a teenage lover.

Mid-June.

Only two days before, Richard had attended another march in an all-day rain. It was a silent protest. Sixty thousand people walking two miles in a steady Seattle drizzle. Masked. Fists raised. Signs streaked in rain-smeared black markers. The only sounds Richard could hear were the rustle of Gore-Tex and a single TV news helicopter overhead. Marching without shouting seemed like the best way to stay safe while protesting during a pandemic.

"Finally," Richard said, as he settled into a chair in his backyard with a freshly poured IPA, his phone tuned into his most recent Road Songs. He liked to critique the flow of his programming, the timing of the mic breaks, the volume levels, and the transitions between songs. Jason Isbell's "Codeine" following Slaid Cleaves' "Broke Down" and leading in to Lori McKenna's "Bible Song."

He tried to read the news. Hate media was calling for the mass arrest of the protesters. Some suggested George Floyd must have had it coming. In the progressive cities, mayors were forming panels to discuss the abolition of police departments. Giant corporations pledged millions of dollars to stamp out systemic racism. Citizens armed with ropes toppled Confederate statues. Aunt Jemima was erased from history.

Richard gazed at the ferns surging from the backyard planters. The clematis feeling along the pathway arbor, up and into gutters and around tree branches. The hostas he had planted years earlier emanated an exuberance he found disturbing, like something out of the Saturday matinees from his childhood that featured giant irradiated ants and mutant spiders.

He was no gardener. He could only plant shrubbery, things to be gazed upon. If it required nurturing it died on his watch. Once he'd received a single bamboo stalk in a clay vase as a gift. A simple plant. It can grow into a jungle, thick enough to conceal rebel armies. He watered it and tenderly rotated it in the sunlight, but it died within a month. Beth, however, planted the lyrics of folk songs. Parsley. Sage. Rosemary. Thyme. She cultivated edible things. Dill. Oregano. Basil. Kale. Chard. Mint. Tomatoes. She was chopping herbs in the kitchen while the broccoli he'd sliced roasted in the oven.

He had walked seven miles that morning. He understood, at some level, that these walks were less about shedding pounds and more about contemplation, that by moving through the streets and alleys and paths of his known world, he remained grounded to his observations. He had seen a caravan of cars rolling along the lake boulevard, balloons affixed to their exterior mirrors and luggage rails. The drivers honked their horns. Another birthday, he'd presumed. There were dark shapes moving through the trees lining the sidewalk. Glimpses of loose black fabric. People in black gowns and black mortarboards. *Ah, high school graduation.* The students gathered at six-foot intervals, waving to the passing cars. Some held signs or flowers. Two of the graduates were hanging out by the water, smoking a joint. The weed would either numb the sadness of this graduation day or it would enhance the farcical nature of the compromise the students were making. It certainly would be a graduation they would never forget, but also a graduation they would most likely want to forget. The effort made by the parents and students was admirable, but the scene, no doubt being enacted across the country, was freighted with absence, like the empty pages of a guestbook at a run-down seaside motel.

Beth's journal.

June 16:

A peaceful Sunday after our birthday evening with Chloe. I think we all had such a good time. Loved that Lummi smoked salmon. I think I was carrying around a lot of angst these days, about, you know, the future of the world and our country and the pandemic and dismantling racism and how we're going to do that. Thinking about my Covid test tomorrow. My first but maybe not my last.

June 17:

This morning: my drive-thru test. I feel fine. Worldwide cases at 7,912,700; deaths at 433,607. U.S. cases at 2,103,990; deaths at 115,762.

June 18:

Test negative. 2 hours ago I took a look at Facebook and saw an AP alert: the Supreme Court upheld DACA, 5-4. Wow. Transgender rights and immigrant rights in the same week.

The Malignancy, itching to get out of the house and kill somebody, held an indoor rally in Tulsa. His first in three months. The arena could hold nineteen thousand people. Four days before the rally, his cultists began lining up outside, like sheep bound for slaughter. The president had them sign waivers absolving his campaign of any liability if they contracted the virus, the virus he still claimed was a hoax. On that same day, new cases of the coronavirus reached their highest level ever in the state of Oklahoma. The president's devotees stayed away in droves. A photograph taken later in Washington captured him walking alone across a neon green lawn, clutching his

MAGA hat like it was a worthless door prize, his face a lump of Napoleonic defeat. His Democratic opponent in the upcoming presidential election was not planning on holding any rallies. He was protecting his health and saving his money, happy to watch his rival cut his own electoral throat as he raged about his declining poll numbers.

Perhaps an assassination wasn't necessary after all, Richard thought. He had to admit it was a baroque solution to begin with, something befitting a cunning and evil czar, not a two-bit, has-been celebrity. Besides, an assassination was a hall pass to martyrdom. Perhaps a medical emergency was a more realistic hope. Something quick and deadly, maybe with a touch of suffering. A stroke would do. Or a good old-fashioned heart attack. Or maybe the president stumbles while extracting his baleen torso from the shower and takes a headlong dive into hard porcelain.

Or he dies like Elvis, sitting on the toilet, Richard jotted in his diary, retweeting bile from QAnon.

On Father's Day, Richard and Beth drove to a campground along Icicle Creek on the east side of the Cascades. The creek, bulging with winter's defrost, squalled down a narrow canyon and flowed into the Wenatchee River in Leavenworth, a town long ignored until the city fathers decided in the 1960s to remake it into a Bavarian village, with half-timbered exteriors, gabled roofs, curlicued moldings, and gingerbread storefronts. The shops sold the kind of knick-knacks you'd find in a traveler's rest stop in the Alps: blonde milkmaids and shepherds wearing painted-on lederhosen. The aggressive tackiness clashed with the surrounding natural wonders of soaring peaks, beckoning forest trails, tumbling streams, and the contemplative quiet of wilderness. The original inhabitants, the Wenatchi Indians (the name means "river flowing out of a canyon"), once fished the confluence of rivers that was considered by their ancestors to be one of the greatest salmon runs in the world.

Campgrounds had reopened throughout the state that weekend.

Richard wanted to sit in his folding chair and sip a beer next to the river. He wanted to hike to a mountain lake. He wanted campfire glow.

Zach and Chloe joined them for a night. They sat around the fire and ate store-roasted chicken, green salad with avocado, tomatoes, pepper jack cheese, and smoked salmon. They toasted Father's Day with a growler of microbrewed pale ale and a drinkable Bordeaux. They consumed chocolate honey grahams for dessert. They talked about murder hornets, large homicidal bees that invaded the native hives of smaller bees and, in an all-out assault, decapitated the swarm in less than an hour. The hornets were supposedly living sixty miles north of where they were camping, apiologists combing the woods searching for their nests. The thumb-sized hornets had inch-long stingers that could feel like a nail embedded in the skin.

"Supposedly, they came from Asia," Richard said.

"Yeah," said Zach, "from China, I heard. Something else sent here to kill us."

"So, yeah," Chloe said, changing the subject, "tomorrow we're going to clear the trail to Snow Lakes and establish, like, safety zones. Then a mule team is going to bring up the dynamite."

"Dynamite?" said Beth, trying not to appear nervous.

"To blow away the unstable sections of a recent rock slide. It's too dangerous for hikers right now, that's why that part of the trail is closed. I might get a chance to blow shit up."

"Do you light a long fuse and then run and hide behind boulders, like in an old Western?" Richard asked.

"No. You just press a button from five hundred feet away."

They finished their dinner, cleaned up and stashed the food in the cooler and put the cooler in the trunk of the car. Sifted the remains of the fire. Brushed their teeth. Stretched. Said goodnight.

He crawled into the tent and fell into an immediate and deep sleep that lasted all of four hours. Thoughts, like caged chimpanzees, began swinging in his mind from one iron bar to the next. He wondered where he had stowed the trail mix. He tried to visualize the exact location of his extra pair of hiking underwear. He made an effort to focus on the muffled roar of the river but could only think of the simmering tension in the country. The protests had eased off, but there were still nightly gatherings, candlelight memorials to George Floyd, the takeover of public streets and squares by activists. Richard began to tabulate and re-tabulate the expected income from their business in the months ahead, adding up the invoices, but then losing track. Eventually, he drifted off for another ninety minutes before waking up at five-thirty. Beth also stirred. They pulled on fleece pants and hats while sitting in the tent and then forced themselves outside. She brewed their coffee. He arranged pine shavings to start a morning campfire.

Chloe was already up, organizing the trunk of her Forester for the day's work ahead. They kissed her goodbye and watched her pull out of the campground at six. Zach stirred and they all relaxed in chairs next to the fire with their morning reading and writing. At seven-thirty, the sun peered over the eastern ridge. The campfire smoke, struck by the rays, hung like translucent curtains in midair.

Zach left to visit his girlfriend in Bellingham and later in the afternoon, Richard and Beth went for a cooling splash in the Wenatchee River, which flowed along a small, sandy beach near downtown Leavenworth. They dried off and set up their camp chairs in the sun. Groups of teenagers and families were spread out around them with beach towels and umbrellas. A woman stood nearby to chat with Beth. No one was wearing a mask, and he and Beth weren't either. They told themselves they were safe in the open air.

He checked the headlines on his phone and saw that things had reached an alarming level.

The global infection rate was now at its highest point so far. Numbers skyrocketing in Texas, Arizona, and Florida. An uptick in the Eastern Washington agricultural town of Yakima, two hours from Leavenworth, where migrant workers harvested fruits and vegetables. The governor issued a new statewide order that masks would now have to be worn in any public areas. Around them were people talking and laughing, hands plunging into bags of tortilla chips, iced lattes sipped through straws, clusters of bodies, river wet, mouths only inches away from other mouths, guffaws and shrieks and an all-encompassing obliviousness. Richard looked at Beth and they quickly gathered up their towels and chairs and returned to their car.

The next morning, they broke camp and drove in the general direction of Seattle, turning down a gravel road near the top of Blewett Pass and parking at the trailhead for Ingalls Creek. They shouldered their packs and tramped away into backcountry solitude for their first overnight hike of the season. After three miles they saw an inviting campsite down by the creek, pitched their tent on a level patch of dirt next to a fire ring, splashed the ice-cold water from the creek on their faces, lodged four beers in an icy pool at the creek's edge, and then hiked on a few more miles with daypacks, traversing shadows, the creek a steady soundtrack, the afternoon heat a dry and tolerable ninety degrees. They lacked the ambition for a longer hike. They wanted to nap in the shade, read by the river, nurse their beers.

Two miles on they came to an immense field of boulders, piled at the bottom of a cliff face that stretched straight up five hundred feet or more. The rocks were the size of house trailers. Richard could feel cold air seeping out from the jagged dark recesses created by the boulders. He knelt down and held out his hands. It was air-conditioner cold. The tumble of gigantic rocks—engineered by glaciers and avalanches and shielded by a stand of evergreens—somehow captured the off-gas of underground water and the downslope breezes and transformed them into an environmental Freon.

Back at camp, they sank their naked bodies into whirlpools fed by the ferocious swell of the creek. He liked to stretch out in swift-flowing streams, grab onto large rocks on the bottom, and submerge his body as if doing a push-up, his head pointing upriver, the icy river washing away the sweat. They lifted their heads from the brain-cleansing cold and tipped them backwards, the water dripping down their backs in rivulets from the tendrils of their pandemic hair. They finished off the beers while reading, and then napped.

Dinner was lasagna and a can of red wine. They poured boiling water into a foil pouch, closed the top, and set a timer for twelve minutes. While waiting for their food to materialize, they stuffed their sleeping pads into lightweight collapsible metal frames, turning their beds into comfortable backcountry chairs. They sat down at river's edge, opened the wine, and passed the food pouch back and forth, each taking two or three forkfuls of the rich, tangy sauce. To someone watching, the way he and Beth ate in the backcountry might look unpalatable. But their method eliminated the need for bowls and after-dinner clean up. Wipe the fork, fold up the pouch, put it into their plastic garbage bag, crush the empty can, done.

The sun had begun its slow collapse and the mosquitoes that had been kept at bay by the afternoon breeze now mounted a voracious assault.

"I wonder if a mosquito's bite could transmit the virus," Richard said. "I mean, you know, they carry malaria, Zika, Dengue fever, smallpox, West Nile, why not the coronavirus?"

"Good question," Beth said. "Google it when we get home."

Dark clouds bruised the sunset. Thinking it might rain, Richard pulled the rainfly over the tent and climbed into his sleeping bag. He closed his eyes and listened to the gossip of the river. High-pitched and giggly. Every now and then he would hear a muffled thump, as boulders were repositioned on the river's bottom. Sometimes it sounded like the deep bass of a car stereo. Before he fell into a blessed eight-hour sleep, he recalled something he'd read about the virus, something about its design. It clarified for him what humans were up against: The virus' only imperative was to survive. It can never be expected to go against its nature.

They awoke to a Marseille sky, a blue cut-out framed by the trees surrounding their campsite. He gathered up wood for a fire while Beth brewed the coffee. She looked at him and chuckled.

"Sorry," she said. "It's your hair."

They were both trying to make good on their pact to not get their hair cut for the duration of the pandemic, but it was stretching on longer than they'd thought it would. While others made appointments at their favorite salons, he and Beth remained half-heartedly committed to the adventure. Her hair was a delicate silver, with a pentimento of blonde and charcoal strands falling around her shoulders and down her back. Her hair had grown straight and lovely. His hair looked like something a squirrel had assembled from the stuffing of a discarded couch.

They ate their breakfast, read their books, and then broke camp. He enjoyed the process of dismantling their portable home, stuffing bags in sacks, rolling up pads, collapsing the tent with its lightweight aluminum poles, its nylon mesh pockets, its polyurethane fabric, the strategically placed windows, the color-coded webbing and buckles. Their palm-sized stove which screwed into the butane canister, their small pot with a folding handle, their sleeping pads which expanded into comfortable beds when inflated and when deflated could be rolled up, reduced to the size of a loaf of bread, and stuffed in a pouch. Their retractable trekking poles, made of NASA-grade titanium, which helped get them up and down the trail on their sixty-plus legs. Their omni-shade hats and convertible pants and sweat-wicking shirts and thin merino socks. Smartwool and Ex-Officio and North Face and Patagonia and Columbia and REI. All of it, when condensed and folded and rolled and stuffed, fit neatly into their backpacks. This was the kind of innovation he was impressed by. Not cryptocurrency and blockchain, not Apple Pay and Venmo, but the ability to carry the basic tools of survival on your back.

They loaded up and started back towards the car. The sun slashed through the trees. Hopeful narratives sifted through his mind: More outings, more hikes, small parties with friends around their backyard campfire.

The virus had forced them to save money. They'd banked a few thousand dollars, and a couple of days ago he'd taken a peek at their retirement accounts and was startled to see they had not lost ground. He didn't know why, really, since he'd never possessed any real conception of the stock market. The averages and the industrials, the Dow and the Nasdaq. When the numbers were announced at the end of every NPR newscast they might as well have been speaking in Urdu. Mutual funds, bonds, high-risk, low-risk. He hadn't a clue. By the end of the last week in June the stock market, whatever that actually was, had made more money than at any point in the last twenty-two years. He had no vocabulary to explain this. But he felt a small measure of peace of mind to know that he and Beth would most likely avoid the fate of spending their final years living in a rusting Winnebago.

On the drive home they stopped in Roslyn, a village tucked in a nook against the left cheek of the Cascades. The town had mastered the mellow vibe common to liberal outposts of the West, where the line between rugged individualism and progressive politics was drawn in locally roasted espresso beans and handcrafted, dry-hopped ales. Inside the Brick, the local watering hole, they looked forward to their first dine-in restaurant experience since the pandemic began, grabbing a table next to a fan placed near the open front door. The owners had marked every other table with a big white X to indicate they were off-limits.

Richard perused the menu, which involved a QR code, the scanning app that he'd heard about years ago but had vigorously avoided, considering it another desecration committed by technology. The waiter stood six feet away and took their order: A bacon burger, shared, with fries. Two draft beers.

While waiting they looked at the headlines and again, the news was harrowing. The country had set another new record for daily infections, more even than the days of late March and early April, when hundreds were dying every day in New York and New Jersey. In Washington state, many counties were progressing through the phases of reopening, following the guidelines established by the governor's task force, but in other states—the southern states—there were no guidelines, only vague, conflicting suggestions and toothless, finger-wagging scolds from local health officials.

The beers arrived, the color of honey, birthed from Yakima hops, and poured from a tap into twenty-ounce glasses, the glass cold and healing on their palms. Then came the burger and fries. The burger was medium rare, the bacon crisp on the edges, its fatty bits hanging out of the bun with a come-hither succulence, a thin slice of cheddar melted over the meat, the bun toasted and crunchy around the rim. The fries were oiled and limp, curled in on themselves like edible grubs. They attacked their meal as though recovering a cherished childhood memory.

Beth napped on the drive down the west slope of Interstate 90 towards Seattle. The radio was on a low murmur. The latest numbers were troubling, not only because they were so unrelenting, but because they also revealed something ugly metastasizing throughout the country: a mean and foolish pride, a type of bullheaded ignorance, and a fuck-you selfishness. This ugliness threatened to render every hour spent in lockdown a wasted sacrifice, threatened to spill over into a violence that would make the skirmishes among the cops and the BLM protesters look like a playground scuffle.

Back home that night, fresh from showers, wearing their pajamas and eating a light salad, they smoked a little ganja in the kitchen and took their plates and wine out to the studio to watch *The Magnificent Ambersons*, Orson Welles' disfigured masterpiece about the spoiled scion of a fading aristocracy, incapable of realizing the world was evolving and modernizing and moving on without him. The movie, set in 1918, did not mention the influenza epidemic raging at the time, but instead depicted the virus of arrogance and entitlement infecting the young brat, George, who everyone pampered and made excuses for. Welles' original intent, a statement on American fecklessness as seen through the myopic lens of privilege, was mutilated by the studio's insistence on a happy ending. But the coruscating essence remained: the portrait of a childish tyrant who lived a life of deluded self-importance.

After the movie, Beth went to bed and Richard stayed up to watch MSNBC. He needed to connect visuals to the audio they'd been hearing on NPR. Certain stories and themes were starting to repeat themselves, like a long-running Broadway show that had replaced its original cast with new actors in the same roles. Emergency room doctors and nurses from red state cities—Houston, Miami, Phoenix

—were now interviewed on the cable news shows, filling in for the desperate doctors and nurses from New York and Boston. They read from the script that had been written in March, made the same desperate pleas for social distancing, mask-wearing, and PPE. They described overcrowded ICU wards and spoke of slow solitary deaths. It was like living in a velodrome, an endless cycling around and around the same landscape, while the president continued to gaslight the populace.

"The United States of America did not ask for this plague and every American has been affected from the closure of our economy to caring for the sick and mourning those tragically lost, but under the leadership of the president our Transition to Greatness has already begun, and the American people are showing tremendous courage to defeat the virus, responsibly open the economy, and restore law and order to our streets," said a press advisor, one of the Children of the Corn the president employed to whitewash his lies and crimes.

Transition to Greatness was an update to the motto—Make America Great Again—that helped him get elected, and a subtle adjustment to the pre-pandemic version, Keep America Great. Never mind that the chronology was confusing. If they already made America great, and were now keeping it great, how could they be transitioning to greatness?

This slough of propaganda never seemed to stop, never seemed to align with reality. It bludgeoned the senses, a daily battering that made sleep, when it came, a deliverance.

12

ENCOUNTER

Hoping to calm the monkeys still scurrying in his brain, Richard tried to read. He opened the book on his bedside table. The author was writing about zoonosis, the spillover of animal infections into human populations. Some African cultures believed viruses were hexes or spells unleashed by evil spirits, punishment for selfishness, hoarding, materialism. These believers lived in remote areas scattered along the banks of torpid rivers. Malarial landscapes like something out of Graham Greene. Maybe the coronavirus was a pox on humanity, for its greed, gluttony, vanity, and vice. Or maybe it was more like revenge, Mother Nature's karmic smackdown. There was evidence that the virus could have originated in a bat whose jungle habitat was disrupted by human encroachment, mining companies or construction crews, throwing the ecosystem out of whack, bringing a creature whose immune system could handle the virus into contact with a human's that could not (this was exactly what was depicted in the final sequence of *Contagion*).

One could make all the Biblical analogies one wanted, construct the literary metaphors, search for mystical meaning, or defer to the timeworn rationalization—*everything happens for a reason*—but the plain truth was that the virus had no agenda, no politics, no ulterior motives. It just happened to announce itself when things were beginning to go pear-shaped in the country anyway, when benevolence and brotherly love were already in short supply, when climate change had reached the level of climate chaos.

Richard knew that if he backslid into the darkness, he might not find his way out again, so he recommitted to his plan: *pay attention, tell about it.* The fragments and phrases and paragraphs he wrote in his journal began to take on shape, a kind of memoir or maybe a novel with himself as the main character, living in a world in which the fantastic and the surreal became commonplace, routine, acceptable.

The United States set a new record for 75,000 positive cases in a single day.

In two weeks, federal unemployment payments were scheduled to end.

A few weeks after that and citizens would be faced with a dilemma: Pay their health insurance bill or buy enough food to make it to the end of August.

He googled whether or not mosquitoes could transmit the virus. The consensus seemed to be that they could not. Something in the RNA stew of the virus was probably not conducive to mosquitoes acting as a carrier, an intermediate host. *Probably not.* There was still so much to learn. Questions of mutation, transmission, spread. Many, many unknowns.

He continued to edit the documentary for The Heiress.

He continued to read and exercise.

He continued to exit the shower and catch glimpses of himself in the mirror as a kind of test to see how much horror he could stand.

. . .

Mornings he spent compiling new music from the internet, building playlists for his radio show, thinking of all the musicians, the singer-songwriters, the acoustic duos and trios and bands, now beholden to the anonymity of music streaming companies for their paltry royalties. No more in-person concerts. No more touring. Many artists were recording protest songs, songs about struggle and resilience, all of them calling for solidarity, but tinged with doubt. By curating music for his listeners, Richard was offering solace and companionship to all who shuffled through these fathomless days. He needed to believe that the music he played might comfort someone in their own darkness.

Their friend Anthony lived in southwest Seattle in a rented two-bedroom cottage with his seventeen-year-old daughter. He made his living as an art therapist for the elderly and the disabled, but he'd stopped seeing his regular clients in person. Now he played and sang cowboy songs on his guitar via FaceTime for housebound seniors. His lack of money was constant. His debt eternal. He owed years' worth of back taxes and, at age sixty-two, was still paying off the college loans for his master's degree. He bought guitars from pawn shops and ate basic pastas. He invited Beth and Richard over for dinner while his daughter was staying at her mother's.

 A few body parts of a chicken were stretched out on the barbecue when Richard and Beth arrived. They drank pale ales and munched the bread Anthony had baked that day. They tore it into chunks and dipped them into peppered olive oil, separated into two small bowls, one for them and one for Anthony. His homemade bread was hit-or-miss, unchewable soft cement or, like this evening, nutty and pliant. Laundry flapped in the breeze on a line extended between two ash trees. Beth broke into the Malbec rosé they'd brought. Richard opened the Cabernet. Anthony showed them the vegetables he'd planted in March. Squash, salad greens, peppers. He'd never been much of a gardener or a cook, so it was encouraging to see him proud of his handiwork. Meanwhile, the chicken overstayed its welcome on the grill.

They shared passages and impressions from the books they were reading—Beth's history of the 1918 influenza pandemic, Anthony's study of the bubonic plague, Richard's book on zoonosis. Eventually, the conversation wound its way to the consuming nightmare.

"The president is a virus," said Anthony.

"Well, I've been writing that he is a cancer," Richard said. "A malignancy. But, yeah, virus works, too."

Beth amplified the personification. "He feeds on the adulation of the crowd. The crowd sustains him. Without the cheering multitudes, he would die."

"He infects them with his bullshit," said Richard. "Eliminate his followers, and he has nowhere to spread. The virus reaches its natural dead end."

"It's like Jim Jones," said Anthony. "He took everyone with him and the cult ceased to exist."

The rallies that provided the Virus with hosts continued to be cancelled, especially after the farce in Tulsa. And the Virus's appearances on TV were so incoherent and unhinged that people shied away when they saw it standing in front of a microphone, its long red tongue dangling to its crotch. The Virus' upcoming convention, scheduled for late August, was a death ship, with even the rats all fleeing. The presidential debates would have to be televised to an empty studio.

Anthony had worked at the same Seattle TV station as Beth and Richard back in the mid-eighties, before moving back to New York for eleven years. Richard would visit him in Manhattan and they'd spend epic days and nights exploring the shelves at Kim's Video, eating Two Boots pizza at one in the morning, smoking dope from noon until the following dawn. Other times he and Beth would fly the red-eye to LaGuardia to visit her college friend who lived in a rent-stabilized apartment in the East Village. The four of them gobbled marijuana cookies and danced at CBGB and breakfasted on rudimentary eggs at the Yaffa Café. In the early part of the century, Richard and Beth screened rough cuts of their documentaries at the Film Forum and caught the attention of distributors. Beth and Anthony both read stories at the Cornelia Street Café, its narrow basement stage a portal to modest acclaim. They all pretended to be artists in the greatest city in the world.

But New York had long ago lost its love for the dreamer. Just that morning, Richard received an email telling him that his essay documentary had been rejected a second time from the same New York organization that had praised it (*impressive! a magnum opus!*) and promised him feedback if he resubmitted the film. But their promise of feedback was a lie. The latest rejection, written in the boilerplate of all rejections, confirmed once and for all that the doors of the city's documentary industry were closed to him. He laughed about it, bitterly, and then spat out a sarcastic return email to the organization's staff. He did not expect a response, yet in writing the email he experienced a rush of brain-pleasing amino acids. New York, the city he used to love for its museums and arthouse cinemas and slatternly taverns, was gone. Kim's Video, gone. The Yaffa, gone. CBGB, gone. Cornelia Street Café, gone too, bum-rushed by real-estate carnivores. In this New York, the young Patti Smith and Robert Mapplethorpe would have died on the streets and been buried in unmarked graves. The city's love of itself, which Richard used to think was endearing, now spoiled his memories. He saw this in the governor's press conferences in March, a kind of one-man show of the city's aggressive self-regard. "We're ground zero for the virus," he boasted. "The canary in the coal mine." True, the deaths in New York were horrendous, but the governor seemed to have forgotten that the pandemic had not begun there. As in everything, he wanted all eyes on himself and his city.

When the number of worldwide infections climbed to 1.5 million new cases a week, Richard retreated to his studio. He clicked to the Criterion Channel to watch *The Roaring Twenties,* a film made in 1939 by the director Raoul Walsh. As the story goes, Walsh lost an eye as a young man when a jackrabbit crashed through his car's windshield. He wore a rakish eye patch and—judging by this film—he had an uncanny knack for narrowing the intensity of his dramas, for a nervy economy in his editing. A classic gangster drama set during Prohibition, the film was a commentary on the wrongheadedness of government-sanctioned morality and the pitiful treatment of World War I veterans returning to an America where the only decent paying jobs involved running bootleg whiskey. The speakeasy scenes were riotous mini-masterpieces, bodies climbing over each other, packed together like tinned fish, alcohol flowing as if from fountains, everyone glistening in carnal sweat. There were fistfights, gunshots, casual murders. The film starred Humphrey Bogart and James Cagney, the actors like two sticks of unstable dynamite jostling in a box. Bogart was mean and murderous. Cagney ruthless and hopped-up. He acted on his toes, bounding across the sets like a springbok. A person could lose weight just by watching him.

After the film—after every film he had watched since the pandemic started—Richard was left with the eerie impression that movies were now the only touchstone to the Before Times, when people played and partied and lived in community with others, face-to-face and body-to-body. How long before a movie could be made again with a crowd scene, with lovers kissing on a dance floor, or with two great actors like Bogie and Cagney snarling nose-to-nose?

The president attempted a reset on his floundering press briefings. For two days he stuck to a written script, delivering dry data in a pouting monotone, taking no questions, and then retreating behind a curtain. But on the third day he was challenged by a reporter for retweeting a video featuring a witch doctor hawking the president's favorite drug, hydroxychloroquine. The doctor had a history of making bizarre claims. She believed the government was run by lizard people, that DNA from aliens was being used in human medicines, that endometriosis was caused by having sex during dreams with witches and demons. The president, annoyed that his idiocy had once again been exposed by the Fake News Media, left the podium without responding to the question. But in his world, a world where he was a very stable genius and a consummate dealmaker and the least racist person you ever knew, it was perfectly rational that over-the-counter pills were manufactured from the cells of Klingons and that pain in the uterus was caused by devil-fucking.

Richard considered including the episode in his book, but it was too imbecilic. No one would believe it.

Beth's journal.

July 20:

Numbers continue their grim trends. Like thermometers gone wild. Like carnival rides. What a mess. What an example for the ages of where hubris + anti-science stupidity + non-leadership can lead us.

Washington is now on New York's quarantine list.

July 24:

I woke up groggy and pummeled by dreams.

July 25:

4,123,600 confirmed cases. 145,430 dead.

July 26:

Just a quick scribble, as we pack up for the Methow (yay!).

It's amazing to think of the terrible sadness of the wildfire smoke 2 years ago. And yet: this year we have the pandemic.

Their hair had become unmanageable. The hair of recluses, off-the-grid weirdos with dial-up and tires on the roof. They made appointments at their salon, all the stylists and their clients double-masked. A small thing, a haircut, but it gave Richard a new sense of forward momentum.

He packed their car for the four-and-a-half-hour drive to the Methow Valley, east of the North Cascades, a playground for hikers and bikers and climbers, where tourists arrived in SUVs topped with sport carriers and bike racks, where families floated down rivers in inner tubes and inflatable canoes, where you could hike to a mountain's ridge in the morning and quench your thirst at a craft brewery in the afternoon. They drove through the North Cascades, the road parting curtain after curtain of mountain ranges.

The cabin they'd rented was set back fifty yards from the river's edge, in a stand of cottonwood, the trees offering shady relief from the heat. They kept the windows and doors closed in the cabin during the day, the blinds lowered, the lights off, to retain the night's cool air. He looked forward to baking in the sun in the afternoon, and then to submerging his body into the cold river. He would climb out, dry in the sun, maybe fifteen minutes at most, move his chair into the shade, and then back into the sun an hour later to bake again, and then another douse. Hot skin. Melted snow. Rocks shimmering like emeralds under the river's scrim.

Zach and Chloe joined them for a few days. She was fresh off her latest Forest Service hitch, working in the backcountry with her boyfriend. Zach had driven over the Cascades from Bellingham, where he'd spent the night with his girlfriend.

They had an insistent need to practice normalcy, or to at least playact its rituals. They hugged and kissed, ignoring the possibility that one of them could have brought the virus with them.

Guilt-free sloth was the only plan. He and Beth would get up three hours before the kids and spend the chilly mornings on the riverbank with black coffee and books, then a morning walk. Zach and Chloe would emerge from nest-like sleep, gather their books and coffee, and arrange themselves in their camp chairs, silent and deep into their reading, the sun now panned further right and craning higher in the sky.

His kids grew up with the texture of paper between their fingers. Zach sprawled across two chairs, with three or four books at the ready. He often kept a notebook handy to jot down ideas, or he wrote reminders in ink on his right palm. Chloe climbed into a book like it was her private treehouse, above the fray. She didn't want to be disturbed.

Before noon, before the heat rendered any exertion a chore, they hiked to the Goat Peak fire lookout, a short but relentless climb. Standing on the lookout's balcony, a person could see Desolation Peak to the west, where Jack Kerouac spent a summer as a firewatcher, writing his mad Zen riffs. The views from Goat Peak were stupendous, but the lookout's actual value was mostly for show. New fire-spotting technologies had long ago made the place obsolete. It was closed for the pandemic. The window shutters banged against the sidewalls, the hatch at the top of the stairs was locked, the balcony off-limits.

The day was clear. They could see Canada.

Richard looked at his grown children and marveled. They had probably first hiked this path when they were ten and seven years old, and here they both were, twenty years later, intact and holding their own. Chloe was sometimes overwhelmed by a swirl of anxieties, but her work in the forests and mountains brought her back to a kind of balance. She'd once posted a picture on Facebook of her and her crew shoring up a trail on a mountainside. She wrote in the caption: *Just another day moving rocks at the office.* Nature was her antidepressant.

They had their good humor, their health, and a confidence that would help them navigate this epoch as if surrender were not an option. They'd come to understand that there were no more givens in the world.

In the afternoons they all snacked on apples and cheese and salami and washed it down with a hoppy ale, pulled from a cooler they kept within arm's length of their chairs. They told silly jokes, ate chips, cracked more beers, and tried to recall the last twenty years of forgettable Best Picture Oscar winners. Richard came up with *The Artist* and *Argo*. Zach added *Slumdog Millionaire* and *Hurt Locker*. Chloe, *Chicago*.

"Hideous. Awful," Richard said. "The death of cinema." There were other abominations he never bothered to see: *Green Book. A Beautiful Mind.*

"*The Shape of Water,*" Beth added. "Talk about death."

They discussed masking and the social distancing of peers. They reviewed the latest infection rates. They wondered aloud if maybe the virus wasn't as serious as the media said it was.

"I mean, is it better to get the disease, suffer a bit, and then come out clean on the other side?" Richard said. "You know, make our contribution to herd immunity?"

They all shook their heads.

"No," Zach said. "I wouldn't wish it on anybody."

"Remember the hospitals," Beth said. "Our contribution should be to not get sick so we don't take up a hospital bed meant for someone who needs it more."

"Agreed," Chloe said. "Plus, you could get it and still feel shitty for weeks."

"You're right. Shortness of breath. Bowel troubles. Mental fogginess." Richard was glad to see they were all in agreement. If Covid was anything like his illness in Mexico, he had no intention of getting that sick again.

"My sense of smell is still off," said Zach. "Smells that I take for granted, that I encounter every day, like the scent of my own body, are altered somehow. I think that I don't smell the same as I used to." They assured him that he smelled fine, but something in his scent receptors, a short in the ganglion, convinced him things weren't the way they should be.

The internet connection at the cabin was spotty, but Beth managed to find a patch of Wi-Fi air space near another house a short walk down the road. They stood there and waited as their phones gobbled up newsfeeds, emails, and texts like piranha. Richard took his phone back to the river's edge to digest. Even here, by the musical river, in the dreamy shade, it was impossible to ignore the slow-rolling calamity.

Fifteen hundred had died yesterday. Fourteen hundred the day before that. The U.S. had only 4 percent of the world's population yet

25 percent of the world's positive cases. The economy had set a record for the speed and severity of its collapse. In three days, unemployment benefits would expire. The president decided this was a good time to tweet that he might delay the election.

Of course. Why not? For the last two years Richard had offered up his prediction that the president would try to cancel or suspend elections, declare martial law, proclaim victory even if he lost. Most of his friends politely scoffed at the prediction, but everyone was coming around to the reality that even some of the president's most vile attempts at authoritarian rule actually had a way of insinuating into the fabric of daily operations: Muslims banned from entering the country. Environmental regulations repealed. Extremist right-wing judges repopulating the nation's courts like the alien pods in *Invasion of the Body Snatchers.*

It was entirely possible the president was deliberately evading taking action to end the pandemic because it was the only thing the media was covering. Behind the scenes, he was dismantling democracy.

A family of ducks negotiated the rapids, twenty yards from where Richard sat. Four toddler ducks, little handfuls of down, were being taught when to float, when to paddle, when to tack right against the current, when to cut a diagonal towards the shore. Their parents flanked the brood, steering them away from rougher waters, and then changed course upstream to force them to swim against the current. They turned back downstream, the ducklings bobbing happily after them, and then cut upstream again. He could watch them for hours, unperturbed as they were by the sickness and bullshit infecting the country.

The sun fell behind the North Cascade peaks and the heat tapered off. They raised the blinds in the cabin, opened the doors and windows, and let the magic-hour light pour in. Dinner was smoked salmon pasta—a family favorite—romaine salad, and fresh-baked French bread from the local grocery store. They gathered at the cabin's dining room table and played a raucous game of Scattergories.

The first letter: A. Things Found in a Hospital. Beth wrote aspirin. Chloe, analgesics. Richard, anesthetic. Zach, amputees.

The second letter: O. Things That Make You Smile. Old friends. Oranges. Orgasms. Orphans.

They argued about word choices. Did Constantinople qualify as a city, even though it had long ago been renamed Istanbul?

The letter M. Things found in the sky: Mist. Moon. Mars. Meteors.

Beth had one of her laughing fits. She was unable to speak, tears forming in the corners of her eyes.

"There is this weird level of all of us getting too used to living this way," Chloe said, as they sat outside on the porch afterward, the sky inking to night, Jupiter and Saturn squinting from the southern void.

"Like, this is how it will be from now on," Beth said.

"Yeah," Zach said. "Will we forget what it meant to go to movie theaters and concerts, have parties, eat at restaurants, sit in a classroom, travel at will?"

This is the way the contagion commanded their lives. It corrupted the ordinary until the corruption became routine, until they all made allowances for it. Every human over thirteen now carried the same two items in their pockets: a smartphone and a mask. Adults conversed with six feet of space between them as though they learned this in early childhood, the way they learned how to share their toys and to say *please* and *thank you*. As they talked, Richard could see his two cloth masks drying on the clothesline, the river softly speaking in tongues behind him.

Their kids left the next morning, Zach to Seattle and Chloe to Leavenworth. He and Beth drove further east towards the Pasayten Wilderness, to hike in a remote northeastern corner of the state.

The road to the trailhead was rutted and narrow, with huge rocks they needed to maneuver around, dead-ending at a large dirt parking lot. He parked their Crosstrek snug up under a tree, hoping to keep the iced-up cooler in the back of the car in shade for as long as possible. They topped up their water bottles, hoisted their backpacks, and began the hike, seven miles through meadows ablaze with orange, yellow, white, blue, and red wildflowers. Purple lupine lined the trail. Alpine larches, their branches burned away in a wildfire two years earlier, flanked them as they climbed to the saddle of Sunny Pass. They stopped there to refuel, leaning against their packs, eating protein bars and orange slices.

The views stretched north to the Canadian border, only a couple of miles away. Other hikers lounged among the rocks and grass. A man they'd met at the trailhead came over to talk. He'd been a Forest Service crew leader in the early seventies, working these hills on months-long hitches, living in a cabin not far from where they stood. He told them about a trapper, a mountain man, who once lived in the region, spending months at a time talking to himself. A hiker found him one day dangling by his neck from a rope looped around a tree branch. He'd left a note saying he was sick and knew he was going to die and he didn't want his body eaten by cougars, so he hung himself to settle the matter. Richard considered this a righteous kind of suicide. Many weeks had passed since he'd last thought of the act, but now he remembered his speculations on rope lengths and pill quantities, splat patterns on pavement, entrance and exit wounds.

"You cold?" Beth said, after the Forest Service man said goodbye.

"No, why?"

"I thought I saw you shiver."

"No, I'm okay." He pushed the visions from his head as they heaved on their packs.

After another mile, they rounded a turn and stopped. A sweeping basin spread out before them, with a brook stitched down the middle. They set up camp on a knoll at seven thousand feet, with a view to the south and a scroll of hills unrolling in the distance. A few clouds trundled across the sky, their shadows like rubbings on the meadows below. He closed his eyes and listened to the aspen leaves whispering in the arbor behind them, the soft nattering of the creek, a bird squeaking, the hum of flies.

The night before, they'd car-camped at a lake nestled into a pocket of the high country. The lake, called Chopaka, was described as an angler's paradise. It was named for a legendary hunter from the Okanagan tribe, who committed some unknown transgression and was turned to stone by Coyote. There were RVs and trailers and rowboats, shaded canopies harboring fishing gear and barbecue grills and portable tables and chairs and flotation devices. It was a primitive campground, with no running water or electricity. Everything had to be brought in by the campers. But despite the diesel-fed vehicles and purring generators, Richard was calmed by the murmur of kids splashing in the lake.

Beth went for a swim. He watched a brigade of electric blue dragonflies hover among the reeds. As dusk crept in, they could hear an oar grazing the metal of a boat in the center of the lake. They allowed themselves to believe they had stumbled into a land that time forgot. The pestilence raged far away, over the hills in another kingdom, one ruled by an insane and syphilitic wizard.

After dinner they took a short walk through the campground, nodding hellos. Moments later a full moon jettisoned from the horizon. Voices quieted. People repositioned chairs for a better view. A saffron reflection of the moon bounced off the water. The campground became as still as stone.

The following evening on their private knoll in the Pasayten, the mosquitoes forced them into their tent, clinging by the dozens to the protective netting.

"I feel like we're mammals in a zoo," Richard said. "One owned and managed and visited by insects."

Beth dug her headlamp out of her backpack and began to read, but was asleep within minutes. He stared at the night sky, the light carving the clouds. He looked again for the show-stopping cameo of the moon. It was up there somewhere, perhaps still blocked by a ridge. As he tried to calculate degrees of orbital mechanics, angles of astronomy and planetary drift, he fluttered off to sleep.

Seven hours later he woke up, relieved he'd slept well. He climbed out of the tent and boiled the water for coffee. The mosquitoes were still sleeping, or maybe they were doing their morning stretches in preparation for an assault. He had on his fleece pants, puffy coat, hat with ear flaps, and his gloves. There was a lovely chill in the air, the kind they could tolerate knowing that in an hour or so the sun would force them to strip down to hiking shorts. He opened two packets of gourmet instant coffee and shook the grounds into their Hydro Flasks, poured in the hot water, stirred, and got back in the tent. They rested their backs against their portable chairs and used their sleeping bags as blankets. They set to reading and writing just as the mosquitoes roused for their morning hunt.

Beth had been writing in journals since she was a young girl. She had volumes stacked on bookshelves in her office at home, hardbacks and softbacks, thousands of unlined pages rich with secrets, self-admonishments, celebrations, and confessions. She often mined this private history for the books she wrote. Richard made notes in his Moleskine: *Sunny Pass. Mountain man. Hanging. Zoo.* The sun began to warm the tent. They kicked off their sleeping bags.

As they hiked back to their car, a wind moaned down the ravine from the pass, its tone warped as it blew through the holes chewed into the charred snags. He felt like they were being followed. One way or another, the wilderness could always freak him out: The dark shadows beyond the border of the campsite. A cracking of branches in the tangle of underbrush off the trail. A glimpse of a furry shape across the river. The appearance of a lone, oddly dressed hiker on the trail, carrying a weapon. Sudden winds, like this one, he imagined were a kind of phantasmal warning.

They reached the trailhead, thirsty and hot. He remembered the peach in their cooler. It was still ice-cold and they took turns biting into it. The juice sluiced down their throats. It was, he decided right there and then, the best thing he'd ever eaten.

They took a different route down from the trailhead, a gravel road running along a river, like a strip of silver fabric threaded through the trees. They passed makeshift campgrounds parked up with trucks and jeeps and Hummers, some with windshield-mounted flags adorned with the underlined names of the president and the vice president and the winning slogan *No More Bullshit*. Flags everywhere, placed strategically atop camper racks or planted temporarily in the dirt. American flags and flags with undiscernible symbols and the occasional Confederate flag (twenty-six hundred miles from Alabama). The people camping stood around smoky fires, sat in chairs and on coolers, eating hot dogs, surrounded by their fortress of vehicles. They turned their heads in unison and stared as he and Beth drove by, like spiders sensing a vibration on their web.

Beth needed to pee, so they pulled off the road and walked a few yards down a woodsy trail, the river sounding like a running tap in the distance. Beth squatted in the bushes. Richard was just about to unzip when he heard a clacking noise, metal on metal.

"Hold it right there, motherfucker."

He looked up. Two figures emerged from further down the trail, their arms stretched out in front of them, one holding a gun with both hands, the other a rifle.

"Richard?" Beth said, quickly pulling up her pants, and stepping out of the bush.

"Just shut the fuck up," one of the men said, as they walked towards them, their weapons obscuring their faces. Richard raised his hands up as if on instinct, something he'd seen countless times in the movies.

"Wait! We're only peeing!" he said, as Beth clutched his arm and dug her nails into his skin.

"I said: Shut. The. Fuck. Up." The men stopped, twenty feet away. They looked maybe in their fifties or sixties, dad-like, with bellies and goatees, their graying hair sprouting from under their trucker hats, one with the president's name emblazoned on it, along with a stitching of the American flag and the year, 2020. The men were draped with gear, gear that to Richard seemed impractical and overwrought: Heavy webbed belts, straps with attached pouches containing flashlights, Velcro pockets holding compasses or GPS doodads, gadgets and thingamabobs dangling from carabiners, sheaths containing large knives strapped over Lee jeans. They both had pistols nestled into holsters under their left armpits, the handles protruding, arranged for easy access by the right hand, like Dirty Harry. The rifle the man held resembled a machine gun, a semiautomatic, maybe an AR something-or-other; the pistol the other man held, pulled from the empty holster on his right hip, looked like the Glock Richard and Zach had practiced with.

The men looked them up and down.

"Are you armed?" The man with the rifle asked.

"No, we're not armed," Beth said, digging her nails deeper. Richard flinched and patted her hand. He flashed back to his thoughts of buying a gun, suddenly relieved he'd decided against it. Without a weapon, he and Beth looked about as threatening as a couple attending a Merchant Ivory retrospective.

"What do you want?" Beth's voice was trembling.

"Who else is with you?" said the man with the 2020 hat.

"No one," Richard blurted and then thought, damn, that was stupid.

"Where is your car?" asked 2020.

"Just back there, on the road. We only stopped to pee." Richard said.

"Shut. Up." The man with the rifle looked around the barrel, squinting at them.

"What the fuck are you doing here?"

"Peeing. I told you. We pulled off to . . ."

"Are you fucking hard of hearing?" the rifleman asked.

Richard was confused. Why did they ask questions if they didn't want to hear the answers? He detected something artificial in the man's tone, something unconvincing, a practiced bravado. What were these guys up to?

"What do you think, Marky?" 2020 said.

Marky? What kind of name is that for a heavily armed backwoods patriot?

"Please, let us go," Beth said, her voice wavering. Richard thought she was jumping the gun a bit. These men weren't really holding them, despite saying "hold it right there." They were more like, maybe, checking them out, as if they'd come upon a couple of trespassers. Why, Richard wondered, were these guys even bothering with them? If 2020 and Marky were Three Percenters taking a little target practice, or hunters doing a bit of out-of-season poaching, or tweakers guarding their meth lab, it seemed like the best course of action would have been to ignore a couple of random hikers taking a leak.

"You're on private property," Marky said, his eyes flitting briefly to 2020.

"Right! Private property," said 2020.

Bullshit, Richard thought, this is federal land. BLM or Forest Service land. Although he had no intention of entering into a public-vs.-private debate with these guys, Richard was getting annoyed. These men were performing, like two comically over-accessorized extras in an Own the Libs marketing video.

"Hey, we're sorry," Richard said. "We didn't see any signs or anything. We'll leave. No problem."

The men exchanged looks.

"Turn around. Walk. Away," said 2020. "Don't come back here."

"We won't," Richard said. "We were just . . ."

"Get the fuck out of here. Now!" said Marky.

"Okay, okay," Beth said, still gripping Richard's arm. They turned back up the trail, walked quickly to the road, jumped in their Crosstrek, and spit up gravel as they drove away.

"Jesus fucking Christ," said Richard, checking his rearview mirror. "You okay?"

"I'm shaking. I don't think I've ever been as scared as I was just then," said Beth.

"Yeah, me too."

"This was scarier than the guy with the knife in Oaxaca. Those guys looked really dangerous."

Richard checked the mirror again, remembering scenes from *Duel,* Spielberg's first film, the malevolent truck that kept appearing in the rearview mirror of the protagonist, moving ever closer, until the film ended in a game of chicken near a desert cliff.

"For some reason I think they only wanted to do just that: scare us," Richard said. Nothing appeared in the mirror except their own dust and the receding forest that had minutes ago seemed so invitingly serene. "They wouldn't have really hurt us or killed us or anything. It would have caused them a fuck-ton of trouble, eventually."

"What was going on, you think? Meth lab?"

"I don't know. They looked too clean. All outfitted like that. It was like they were wearing costumes. Maybe that trail leads to some paramilitary camp or something, and those guys are the guards."

The road broke free of the trees and descended to an open plain. They could see a ranch house in the distance.

"Jesus. I'm suddenly starving," Richard said.

"I think I got pee on my underwear," Beth said, shifting in her seat. "I wasn't finished yet when I heard that noise. That was a gun cocking, right?"

"Yeah. I assume."

"And when I saw them the only thing I was thinking was I've got to pull my pants up as quickly as possible."

"Do you want me to pull over so you can change?"

"Are you out of your fucking mind?"

They drove into the Eastern-Washington prairie town of Tonasket. There was a natural food co-op off the main street where they wandered the aisles looking for something that could qualify as lunch. The store had a deli counter, but it was closed for the day. Next, they considered a café with shady outdoor tables, but the tables were too close together, and the restaurant displayed a campaign sign for a local sheriff running for governor, a gun-toting pandemic-denier who hated government overreach.

"Jesus, I can't eat there." Beth said.

"I read about that guy," Richard added. "He tried to cover up for some friend who had apparently assaulted an underage girl. And this is the sheriff!"

"I don't see anybody wearing masks," Beth said. "Wait. There's a food truck."

Pedro's Tacos was parked in the gravel lot of a closed car-repair shop. It seemed like a better option than the one chain restaurant in the town, a Subway.

"I'm up for that."

Richard hooked his mask around his ears and ordered two tacos and a spicy pork torta from a man they figured was probably Pedro himself. He leaned over the van's warm vats, scooping the meat and lettuce and guacamole into the tortillas and onto the bolillos, the delicious bread that absorbed the rich juices from the slow-cooked pork. They decided not to make a fuss about Pedro's lack of a mask or gloves or hand sanitizer. They also decided to not call the police and report the backwoods patriots who threatened to kill them. It would take hours and lead nowhere.

Pedro handed them their order. Richard wanted to believe the food would be fine. The virus was a respiratory disease, after all; it lodged in the airways, the nasal passages, the lung tissue. This cheap and inviting lunch—he could smell the singed pork and the grilled chicken folded into the tacos—would go directly to their stomachs. Once there, he imagined, all of their gut acids would attack any of Pedro's viral droplets with the ferocity of Pancho Villa.

They ate the sandwiches in the car, washing them down with a couple of Johnny Utahs from their cooler as they drove. The icy beers were like medicine, stinging their throats and calming their nerves. They passed through Omak, famous for the annual rodeo and horse race, the Omak Stampede, that culminated in a plunge down a sheer dirt hillside. It was the city's main tourist draw of the summer, now cancelled. They made another stop, this one for iced Americanos at a supermarket in the county seat of Okanogan. The town's main street was a stretch of squat one-story buildings that sagged in the heat. Many were closed or abandoned.

In the store, he waited at the espresso bar while Beth changed in the restroom. The young woman behind the counter worked at filling three previous orders of jumbo drinks laden with syrups and cold coffee. The process involved trowels of ice and repeated blasts of sweetened juice and multiple shot glasses of espresso and endless ear-splitting grinds of the blender. It took so long that Richard was sure new species had been discovered in the Amazon, Greenland ice shelves had calved into the Atlantic, and several planets had exploded into stars. Standing behind him were three clerks chatting at their cash registers during a customer lull, their masks hanging off their ears. A woman waited in the coffee line with her mask pulled down under her chin. Her companion also stood with her mask covering her mouth but not her nose. She looked to have some kind of disability, her legs and arms too short for her adult-sized body. She held onto a walker.

The barista, a young Latina, was properly masked, but the clientele and her older white workmates casually flaunted the safety guidelines, not caring that this young woman probably returned home to an extended family of parents and grandparents and aunts and uncles who worked in fields and fruit warehouses and numbered among the most vulnerable in the state for catching the virus.

Finally, after one last pulverizing gnash from the blender, the barista sludged the coagulated pink glop of sugar and caffeine into three twenty-ounce plastic cups. The customer rummaged among the wilderness of her purse for a bank card.

Richard ordered their Americanos. Beth came back and stood next to him.

"We should remember what day this is," she said. "If we start showing symptoms in two, five, seven days, I bet we can trace it to this afternoon."

The adrenaline rush of their run-in with the playacting paramilitaries or poachers or tweakers or whatever they were had now worn off. Beth fell asleep after drinking only a couple sips from her iced coffee. He scrolled through his iPod to the playlist he was working on for next week's Road Songs, clicked on shuffle, and heard the rich guitar pluck of Guy Clark's "The Dark" emanating from the car speakers. He drove toward the western sky, Earth slowly turning its face from the sun.

13

PALL

Masked marketgoers in Chittagong.
    Bottles of hand sanitizer in Ankara.
    A crowded hospital hallway in Lagos.
    Subway riders in Xochimilco.
    Cardboard caskets in Guayaquil.

Richard swiped from one photograph to the next in the *Times*' front-page slideshow.

A close-up of hands sewing masks in Pristina, Kosovo.
    Masked soldiers leaning on machine-gun turrets in Democratic Republic of Congo.
    Newborns and their masked mothers in a maternity ward in Manila.
    A public health campaign mural in Medan, Indonesia, the virus depicted as a slobbering green monster.

. . .

The pictures were a kind of ministration. It helped to know that at least everyone on the planet was in this thing together. It was now late summer.

Later that day, the death toll in the United States reached 165,000.

The next afternoon, the Democratic candidate for president and his running mate, the Black female senator from California, delivered speeches to a TV camera in an empty, silent gymnasium. The speeches were read without the usual interruptions of rote applause or cheers or standing ovations. There were no melodramatic pauses or lines orated for live audience impact. The lack of dreary pro forma political theatrics lent a focusing effect to their messages, as though they were sending a rescue flare to America—*help is on the way*—laying out the consequences of another four years if the current occupant in the Oval Office were to win—or, more likely, to steal—the upcoming election.

The first edit of the teaser for the film Richard was making for The Heiress was almost done. He evened out the audio levels, made adjustments to the color, darkened the blacks in some scenes, added the chirp of birds to shots of a forest. Shelley came over in the afternoon to review it. They hadn't seen each other for months. She lived alone with her cat in a mid-fifties brick rambler in West Seattle and had only been out of the house a couple of times since they'd returned from Georgia. They sat in his studio with the door wide open, encouraging the circulation of air, and watched the twenty-minute cut. They both felt the pang of the stalled project, but they were excited to see that the material seemed to be working. It was personal, funny, eccentric. Richard didn't want to be credited as a codirector, figuring the film would have a better chance at festivals with a woman at the helm.

"Do you want a glass of wine?" he asked Shelley, when they moved into the backyard to critique the teaser.

"I'd love one!" she said. "I haven't had a drink all summer."

"Really? That's too bad."

"I realized I can't drink when I'm alone at home. Too dangerous."

Beth poured herself and Shelley cold glasses of white. Richard sipped a pale ale.

"Oh, that's good," said Shelley, closing her eyes as the wine trickled down her throat. "Thank you."

It was clear to them they would need more footage from Sapelo Island and that they would need to make a trip to Brittany to research images and documents to support Shelley's search for her Royalist ancestors. The thought of flying on a commercial airline ignited the ember of panic in the pit of Richard's stomach.

"Is it worth the risk?" he asked her.

"No, not yet."

"They're saying flying might be safe," Beth said. "But what do they know, really?"

There was, so far, little evidence that passengers were contracting the virus. The airlines themselves, some of them at least, seemed to be rigorously enforcing their safety policies. Temperature checks. Masks. Empty seats between passengers. Fresh, circulated air every three minutes.

"Maybe it wouldn't be so bad," Richard said.

The island where much of the documentary was filmed was nearly deserted year-round, as if an earlier plague had denuded it of all except the sturdiest of creatures. Wild pigs and cattle. Buzzards. Biting midges. Live oaks. The island offered asylum from the contagion, and a change of scene. He could busy himself with filming from the list of shots they needed to fill out the story, material he'd missed on their previous two visits. A sojourn in Brittany would offer diversions as well. It would certainly require a side trip to Paris. He daydreamed about sitting at an outdoor table at Le Consulat in Montmartre, surrounded by the chatter of nations, observing the tourist throng in all its herd immunity.

Hard Times in Babylon

"Maybe next year?" he said. "September of next year. Next year, this might all be behind us. You think?"

He poured Shelley another glass.

"Oh God, this is so good," she said.

The next morning Richard woke up with a slight tightness in his chest and the barest hint of a tickle in his nose. It had been more than seven days since he had eaten the torta from the taco van, since their encounter with the two LARPing gunmen. He took a few deep breaths and coughed intentionally to detect congestion or phlegm. Several times in the last few months he had felt the faint stirrings of a cold, followed by a sting of measurable alarm, and then, within minutes, he'd forget all about it and go on with his day. Was this just another case of coronavirus hypochondria? His mind flashed ahead to visions of languishing in bed for weeks, attempting to watch the delayed NBA playoffs within the grip of a murky brain haze, too exhausted to walk the twenty feet to the bathroom, urinating in a milk jug, waiting for Beth's gentle knock at the door, her tiptoeing in wearing a mask, carrying a tray of plain toast, bananas, and liquids containing electrolytes. Would he know with absolute certainty when she should call the ambulance? When his breathing had reached its end game?

These thoughts consumed him for the several minutes he spent putting on his pajamas, rinsing his face with cold water, and walking downstairs for his coffee, which Beth had already made. They kissed—maybe not a great idea if he was sick—and he mentioned the tickle in his throat.

"The virus is raping my cells as we speak."

"Maybe you should get tested," Beth said, "although you're probably fine."

He probably was fine, but he also felt a sense of duty in the idea of getting tested, as though he needed to experience it as a pandemic rite of passage. It was part of his mission—*tell about it*—to stand in solidarity with the millions who had already had a foot-long swab shoved up to their occipital lobe. He'd heard that it hurt, that it felt like a piece of your brain was being plucked out for the microscope.

That afternoon, when he pulled into the testing site in the garage of his HMO, he expected a massive line of cars and a long wait, based on pictures he'd seen on the news. But there was only a single car ahead of him. When it was his turn, a young man in scrubs, a nurse or technician, wearing a face shield, confirmed Richard's member number and then, after explaining the procedure, stuck the first inch of a six-inch swab into each nostril, swiping it around the interior but never penetrating deeper than the bridge of his nose. Richard was relieved, but also disappointed. Did this count as his tour of duty, his Purple Heart?

The swab was deposited into a bag, and he was told he would have his results within 24 hours. In the morning, he checked online and was relieved to see he was negative. It became an anticlimactic footnote in the book he was writing.

The days shortened, the sun hunkering lower in the sky, more of a lateral move above the horizon, illuminating the understory of the trees in his backyard bower. People were resigned to spending the oncoming fall and winter in hibernation.

Jobless days.

Virtual learning.

Holidays celebrated in absentia.

Beth's journal.
August 23:
US-5,681,400 infections. 176,200 deaths.
God? Please. Help.

The following Monday, the Republican convention began.
If Richard had just awakened from a four-year-long coma and tuned in

to the television broadcast, he wrote, *he would have thought he was watching sneak previews of a new miniseries, a satirical montage delivered with sneering outrage, surrounded by over-the-top art design, and starring a rotund creature of comic monstrosity, all of it assembled into a debauched prime-time spectacle. The president's wife gave a speech, the Slovenian-American with the smoldering scowl of the model she once was, her narrowed eyes disguising the vacant lot of her personality. She appeared to have only accomplished two things in her life. One was birthing a son, and the other was posing in the swimsuit edition of Sports Illustrated wearing a string bikini and hugging a six-foot inflatable whale. She read from a teleprompter, in a fractured Boris-and-Natasha kind of English, her head swiveling from right to left, left to right, straight ahead, and then right again. Was she controlled by invisible wires? She talked about the evils of social media and her love of her son, the now-gawky teenager who, when standing with his family in public, looked like a victim of Stockholm Syndrome. She mentioned those felled by the virus as if ticking off a list of remaindered items from a Nordstrom Rack sale. She spoke of the decency and honesty and authenticity of her husband. She spoke of his love for all Americans, his dedication to working hard on their behalf. There were cutaways to the president, sitting in the front row, surrounded by his maskless disciples, listening to his wife describe a person he didn't recognize and had no hope of ever becoming.*

The entire display was worthy of imperialist dynasties, staged at the White House in clear violation of several laws prohibiting the use of federal property for election campaigning. The president and his retinue of grifters were announcing to the world that they would tell any lies in order to stay in power.

Richard reconsidered buying a gun. After all, did he want to be one of the millions of Americans staring at their television screens the day after the election, dumbfounded and aghast, as armed militiamen rode the streets in their two-ton Chevy trucks, the country as lawless as Yemen, with nothing but a pair of trekking poles to defend himself?

. . .

Masked shoppers in Ashdod, Israel.
    Socially distanced college students in Rome.
    A Bolivian grandmother sobbing in a cemetery in La Paz.

By nightfall on the West Coast, the U.S. had surpassed 185,000 deaths and tallied more than six million positive cases. Beth had decided to stop writing down the numbers in her journal. "I started keeping track because I wanted to see the numbers go down, not up," she told Richard. "It's too depressing."

They fled back into the wilderness for one more night out, scrambling in early September heat over roots and boulders to Lila Lake, burrowed among rocky knolls in the Alpine Lakes region of the Cascades. On a ledge above the shore they erected their tent, leaving the mesh ceiling open to the sky, and inflated their pads and spread out their sleeping bags and camp pillows. Beth gathered up their depleted water bottles and he carried the water filter and its rubber bladder to the edge of the lake. He submerged the bladder and watched it fill, then he screwed on the filter, and squeezed the cold water through the filter into their bottles. Parched from the hot four-hour hike, they guzzled, stripped off their clothes, dove into the lake, and allowed Lila to wash the sweat from their bodies. They dried themselves on the bank and changed into their clean warm clothes for the coming evening. On the ledge, they read their books while shadows dilated across the lake below them, their dinner of Kathmandu Curry cooking in its foil pouch, the setting sun behind them splashing a crimson wash against the western face of Hibox Mountain, the bald spire directly east of their ridgetop balcony.

    "Tough climb," Beth said. "But man, it was worth it."
    "Yeah, for a while there I thought it would never end."
    "How many hundreds of feet was it?"

He pulled out his phone and checked the altimeter. "Looks like we climbed around twenty-eight hundred."

Two tents were set up on the opposite shore of the lake. A barely audible echo of a conversation reverberated off the still water.

"Looks like those folks have a sunset view," he said.

"Should we be over there instead?" Beth asked. There were always calculations to be made in picking a campsite.

"I like the way the light is hitting that spire," he said. "And in the morning, we'll get the sunrise."

"I'm happy here," said Beth.

They finished their dinner and tidied up the camp. Richard walked to the edge of the rim and soaked in their private view. What he loved most about the natural world was its immortal ruthlessness. Its instinct for survival. Its utter indifference to the humans who walked within it. Nature existed outside of human need and want. A glassed lake in the lap of a mountain. A tumble of rocks left behind by an ancient glacier. A torrent of water cleaving the earth. Nature responded to civilization's relentless assault upon its water and air and earth with a violent defense, wielding weapons of storm, avalanche, drought, and fire. Beauty and terror in perpetual coupling. Nothing could kill it. Earthlings were at its mercy.

They retreated with their chairs into the tent, snug in their sleeping bags, reading with their headlamps. Now and then he looked up at the darkening blue, marking the seasonal advance of an earlier night.

Two hours later, the full moon peered out from the edge of the mountain and began its trek upwards, spilling an otherworldly, blood-orange reflection across the alpine plateau. "There must be a fire somewhere," Beth said.

They awoke a few minutes before sunrise, a light brown haze cutting the light. They sat with their coffee, ate their freeze-dried granola, and decided to head back down the trail early while the air was still cool. As they descended, the haze grew thicker, eventually obscuring the sun.

Back home, Richard hosed the dried sweat off their backpacks and hung them out to dry in the afternoon heat. There was the smell of woodsmoke in the air, the sky now a deep yellow in the Cascade foothills. The local NPR station reported that wildfires were burning out of control not only in the brittle grasses and cluttered forests of Eastern Washington, but also in Oregon and Northern California. Hundreds of thousands of acres had gone up in flames within hours, firefighting crews flocking to them like moths.

A one-year-old boy perished in his parent's arms as they tried to flee the inferno obliterating their prairie village.

Small towns south of Portland were evacuated.

The hillsides north of Santa Rosa burned.

And in Yucaipa a blaze erupted when people set off fireworks during a gender-reveal party.

"A what?" Richard asked Beth. "What the fuck is a gender-reveal party?"

Beth guessed that maybe these parties were a kind of protest against the liberal wave of gender-fluid identity politics. Or maybe they're part of some trend designed to feed the insatiable appetite of Instagram. It puzzled him as to why parents were willing to spend thousands of dollars on parties and pyrotechnics to celebrate an involuntary function of biology. Besides, a kid is going to decide for themselves one day if they are a he, a she, a them, an it, or perhaps a gender that had yet to be invented. Why spend a fortune announcing your baby's sex to the world if it might come back to bite you on the ass?

During Beth's first delivery, they'd told the nurses it would be Chloe if it was a girl and Zach if it was a boy. When the baby emerged, someone said, "It's a Chloe!" Richard looked at the puffy pink mass of flesh where his baby's face should be and for a split second he was horrified that his daughter had been born without eyes or a nose. Then he held her and watched with relief as her beauty unwrinkled in his arms. When Beth was pregnant with Zach, she went in for amnio and learned they were going to have a boy. She called Richard in Hawaii, where he was filming for a travel agency, and he remembered his heart vaulting up behind his eyeballs, pushing out tears. No party necessary, just a private whispered celebration.

More than twenty thousand people had to flee their homes after the gender-reveal fire became a conflagration. None of the news reports bothered to mention the baby's sex.

Smoke from the fires gathered into a plume that spun its way to Seattle, blotting out the sun. The sky the color of roasted carrots. Everyone was ordered to stay inside their homes, close their windows, refrain from outdoor exercise. Richard could only laugh at the irony. Another plague, a kind of Biblical asterisk to the pandemic. First a virus, then fire. He next expected a rain of frogs.

The cauterized air bit into their lungs.

Beth had tried to find air purifiers at Lowe's and Bed Bath & Beyond, but the shelves were already emptied. She ordered two of them online, but they wouldn't arrive for weeks. Typical, Richard thought. We'll buy devices to plug into walls, to suck even more energy from the planet, and then we'll be shocked when Mother Earth finally slips our eviction notice under the door.

By Friday more than three million acres were burning in California. A photograph from a farmer's market in San Francisco showed people wearing jackets and masks at midday, the sun exiled beyond a soot-filled sky. Oregon towns he'd never heard of—Talent, Detroit, Phoenix—were scorched to cinders. Dozens of people dead. Many more missing. As the week came to an end, the late-afternoon sun struggled to cut through the fires' gauzy residue. The air quality was rated as "very unhealthy." The streets empty. The small central park in their neighborhood deserted. The next morning: a gesso sky. The air dense with incinerated memories, the pulverized detritus of photo albums, sports trophies, mattresses, wood siding, Sheetrock, plastic toys, linens, clothing, appliances, computer parts, paint from cars, animal carcasses. The AQI, the official Air Quality Index, crept upwards like a fever. 169 to 211 to 241. From Unhealthy to Very Unhealthy. Red to Purple. The air in Seattle was less than sixty notches from Hazardous, which began at 300 and stretched onward to infinity. Maroon was the last color on the chart, the color of asphyxiation.

He tried to distract himself by watching the NBA postseason games, played in the virus-free Valhalla of The Bubble at Walt Disney World in Orlando. There was a fresh and ferocious energy among the players. They'd rediscovered the game's essence, its fluid mechanics. Players no longer had to contend with jet lag and the field operations of flight schedules, baggage claim, ground transportation, new hotels, and unfamiliar bedsheets. They greeted their opponents with bonhomie. They ate gourmet food prepared on-site. They woke every morning to Florida sunshine. It was like summer camp for millionaires. Without a live audience, the players felt little urge to preen and grandstand. It was all about the run, mere mortals suspending gravity and hurling spinning orbs through silk.

After dinner one night, the windows shut tight, and Beth stretched out in the living room to read, Richard filled his pipe with a few hits of Garlic Breath Black Cat and settled in the studio for one of his guilty pleasures, David Cronenberg's *The Fly,* a heartbreaking love story in the guise of a gross-out monster movie. It charts the rise and fall of an inventor, Seth Brundle, an egghead oddball who falls in love with a brainy, sexy journalist and takes her to his apartment to show off his latest invention: two human-sized pods, one that will dissolve all of his body's molecules, and the other, an identical chamber across the room, that will reconstitute those molecules, *Star Trek*-like, essentially teleporting him invisibly through space and time. After a drunken snit of mistaken jealousy, he decides to put himself into the pod. Moments before the crucial flip of the switch, a house fly—which he fails to notice—enters the chamber with him.

When Brundle emerges from the pod, alive and in one piece, he believes he has it all, a world-conquering invention and the girl of his dreams. But soon, very soon, his behavior changes. He grows arrogant and angry. His face is covered with dark splotches. He develops inhuman strength and gymnastic flexibility. Coarse and rigid hairs grow out of his flesh. His girlfriend has one of the hairs examined and they learn the horrible truth: It contains the DNA of an insect.

Preposterous stuff, based on the black-and-white fifties original, but the actors, Jeff Goldblum and Geena Davis, invest the material first with savvy chemistry and then, as Goldblum deteriorates, with a stark and palpable grief. They must confront an intruder within the genetic folds of his body, and then face down existence in an altered realm of being. The film always left Richard feeling haunted.

As he got ready for bed later, he ingested a dropper of tincture, complementing the slight buzz carried over from the Garlic Breath Black Cat. The tinctures—each with a five-to-one ratio of CBD to THC—were called Fairy Wind and Ceres, names that offered pillowy guarantees of slumber. He dripped the oiled liquid under his tongue, bathing the strip of tissue running from the floor of the mouth to the tongue's underside—the *lingual frenulum,* he learned, after googling it —where it was absorbed into the membranes of his mouth. It was not intended to get him high, only to hush the buzzing fly of his anxieties. He lay down and within minutes fell asleep, as if hypnotized by the pendulum of the tilted world.

The next morning, a Sunday, the sky resembled a Cy Twombly abstract, with its scrape of dirtied white chalk against a wall of granite. Richard tried sitting outside, scrolling the *Times'* slideshow while sucking at the carbonized air. Microscopic flecks of smoke could slip past the body's defenses and lodge in the lungs like a vagrant hiding in a crawlspace. Masks, apparently, were useless against anything smaller in size than 2.5 microns, which the dictionary said were equal to one millionth of a meter. He took slow, shallow breaths while listening to his ambient playlist, the swelling drones conjuring up images of orcas breaching the surface of the Pacific.

Masked dancers in an outdoor exercise class in Cape Town.

A line of five men in white Tyvek suits firing rifles into the air in Jakarta.

Wary evening sightseers in Wuhan.

A Covid testing site in San Francisco.

Cardboard cutouts of baseball fans in Seattle.

While the smoke emulsified the western skies, the contagion continued to surge throughout the country. Now: nearly two hundred thousand dead.

Toots Hibbert, the founder of Toots and the Maytals, had died of Covid three days earlier. Some say he coined the term "reggae." Richard listened to *Funky Kingston* while watching the Seattle Storm play their final game of the regular season before moving on to the playoffs, Sue Bird draining jumpers from the left of the key.

.

A package of fifty postcards arrived in the mail, each imprinted with an American flag and the word VOTE stamped across it. He and Beth sat down and handwrote encouraging notes to anonymous Democratic voters in North Carolina, urging them to sign up for mail-in ballots. It was all they could think of to do, in addition to their small monthly donations to various causes. Perhaps the postcard he wrote to a lone shut-in in Raleigh-Durham would be the *one single vote* that saved their democracy. There were forty-six days to go before election night.

Nothing seemed to make a dent in the president's popularity. An investigative reporter produced audio tapes of the president admitting he knew the deadly severity of the virus way back in January, and that he concealed this truth from the American public, telling them instead that the virus would disappear like a miracle. The president claimed he lied because he didn't want to create a panic. *This of course is the same president,* Richard wrote, *who has spent nearly four years spreading nothing but panic among his supporters, braying about Salvadoran gangs slaughtering their teenage daughters, black-hooded antifa hordes burning their cities, Black Lives Matter terrorists laying waste to their suburbs, and Democrats confiscating their guns, indoctrinating their children into socialist groupthink, and strapping them to chairs and forcing them to watch MSNBC with toothpicks holding open their eyelids.*

The zombie horde didn't care. To them, the president's every critic was a liar and his every scandal a hoax.

The forecast finally changed, predicting rain that afternoon. Richard wanted nothing more than to stand in a downpour with his face to the lashing rain and his arms outstretched, like Matthew McConaughey in one of his regrettable romantic comedies. There was a small drizzle at four that helped to partially dilute the skies. He imagined the air was now like wet ash, but when he went out for a walk it smelled cleaner than it had in a week. The AQI had dropped well below 150. A wind kicked up.

He plugged into his iPod and shuffled through songs about alcoholic lovers and lonely women in roadside bars. George Jones sang that he needed the four walls of a tavern around him at all times to keep him from going insane. Not an altogether bad place to ride out a pandemic.

Thirty minutes into his walk, muffled dings began to emanate from his pants pocket. He checked his phone. A text from Beth: *Oh my God.*

He scrolled up to read the previous text from Chloe: *Just heard the news ... trying not to be terrified.*

What news? He scrolled above his daughter's text and saw the link she'd forwarded from the *Times*: RBG dead at eighty-seven.

"Fuck me," he said aloud.

People had come to believe the Supreme Court judge was invincible, unkillable, like Stephen Hawking or Yoda, despite the visible evidence from the last decade that she was shrinking before the nation's eyes. Her death was certainly no surprise, but the timing of it couldn't have been worse. The judge's body had barely cooled before the GOP announced they would confirm her replacement within days of the president's pick, giving the conservatives a six-to-three advantage. The Senate majority leader, who had a septic tank where his heart should be, would consider this his greatest triumph.

The rain finally arrived in full, ending the ten-day siege of smoky skies.

Meanwhile... *meanwhile*... those two hundred thousand deaths.

Beth was already deep into her first phase of REM when Richard came to bed. He nudged his phone awake, checked a few headlines, and then read stories of the dead:

The forty-five-year-old firefighter.

The twenty-nine-year-old caregiver for special needs clients.

The forty-nine-year-old former member of the Temptations.

The twenty-nine-year-old hockey player.

The one-hundred-and-two-year-old former first lady of Costa Rica, who'd fled her staid life in Alabama and married the future president of that country, and who had been born during the 1918 influenza pandemic.

The teacher, the mayor, the journalist, the ballet dancer, the activist, the lawyer, the judge, the ophthalmologist.

The Holocaust survivor, the deejay, the cop, the married couple—together for fifty-three years—who died within minutes of each other.

And the young Broadway actor with a wife and new baby who contracted the virus early on, whose leg was amputated in April due to blood clots, and who suffered in the hospital before dying in July. These were a few of the two hundred thousand. Only a few. What percentage of that cataclysmic tally could be considered victims of the president's negligent homicide?

Before shutting down his phone, Richard tapped a graph on the home screen of the *Times* that represented the country's deaths since March. It resembled a mountain range, with a low peak in early spring, followed by a slight dip and a leveling off, and then a stiff climb in early summer, with another mild descent toward the end of August. Only one week ago, a plateau. Now another peak rose to the right of the graph as the death rate topped one thousand or more every day. Another mountain awaited off-screen, an El Capitan of deaths, with the nation hellbent on scaling it.

Sitting down to his computer the next morning, Richard downloaded digital photos of a dead boy and the boy's family into Final Cut Pro. He was beginning the edit of a video for an organization that raised funds for the counseling of children who'd suddenly lost a parent or sibling. He and Beth had worked for the client for five years. The stories were always sad, but this one was especially so, the death of a ten-year-old from cancer. "I can barely function," his mother said in an interview, "but I'm not alone." She began to cry on camera. "We are living in a world shattered by grief."

He assigned labels to the photos and dragged them into a bin, moved the interview clips into a subfolder, searched through his files of production music and deposited a few tracks into another bin. But he wasn't ready yet to start the actual process of stitching the pieces together, packaging the family's tragic story into a tidy but moving three-minute ask for money.

He saved the file and opened the *Washington Post*. A box in the upper left quadrant of the home screen caught his attention. The box displayed a live camera feed from the nomination ceremony for the new Supreme Court justice in the Rose Garden. It was a sunny day in D.C. and the president had just left the podium, where he'd announced his choice: A white female Catholic conservative with seven children, two of them adoptees from Haiti. A picture showed the children grouped in front of their parents, the five shiny white ones flanked by the two deeply Black ones, like souvenir bookends from an exotic vacation. The justice herself had the straight, shoulder-length hair and the trim middle-age body the president seemed to favor in the women he kept around him. After her brief speech at the podium, she followed the president's entourage into the White House.

The live camera captured, in one long unbroken shot, a soirée of maskless grandees shaking hands and hugging and speaking within inches of each other's faces. Senators and representatives and White House aides. The young, the old, the powerful and the rich. They were smiling and laughing in the September sunshine. They slapped backs and laid affectionate hands on friendly shoulders. Some spoke in conspiratorial whispers. The shot had the feel of live surveillance footage of a group of beings from a parallel universe, and Richard could feel the nausea rise in his stomach. The president and his handlers acted as if they had the upcoming election buttoned up, as if they knew the actual process of voting, of counting the ballots, was only a charade, a bit of theater. They seemed bedazzled by the success of their four-year-long mindfuck of the president's cult. The president had been claiming for weeks the election would be fraudulent, that even if his opponent won in an electoral-college landslide he would not accept the results. This is why they were rushing the confirmation of the Supreme Court nominee, to ensure the court would install the president in the White House, voters be damned. The people at the ceremony all seemed to be in on the plot. They all behaved as though the law and the virus could not touch them, as if they were protected by some kind of magic shield.

14

UNVEILING

Richard's journal was now a furious collection of field notes:

—*A barrage of insults and interruptions from the president during the presidential debate. His hostility is operatic; his orange skin looks as though it could burst like a supernova.*

—*The president tests positive for the coronavirus. Please, please, let the motherfucker die.*

—*A phalanx of doctors marches to an outdoor podium to address the press. They wear white coats over green scrubs, hands clasped in front, with matching masks in pale hospital blue, standing in a rigid V formation, like the choreographed robots in* Metropolis. *They refuse to say when the president tested positive, or who and how many he could have infected.*

—*Within days, others test positive: His closest aide. His campaign chairman. Three senators. His press secretary. Her assistants. And his main speechwriter, the president's Mengele, the architect of his cruel immigration purges, who advocated for the caging of children, a man so reviled that people are willing to accept his demise as a consolation prize if the president survives. Many of the sick attended the event in the Rose Garden, that petri dish of white conservative bodies.*

—*The president is pumped full of steroids, sent back to the White House. He disembarks from Marine One and climbs a set of stairs to a* second-floor balcony, faces the adoring masses on Pennsylvania Avenue, removes his mask and—noticeably wheezing—basks in the foamy hot bath of his triumph. He calls his infection a blessing from God. He crows and boasts and beats his chests with both fists like a bottom-of-the-bill Tarzan.

—Ten days to go before clocks will be turned back.

—Neighbors erect white-roofed canopies over patios. New propane heaters are hauled into yards. Restaurants arrange tables under large outdoor awnings, as though preparing to feed soldiers returning from war.

—Richard buys three large bags full of New Mexican piñon to burn in the chiminea during the cold evenings of the coming months. The wood burns clean and smells like a Navajo campfire.

—Abdul is very worried. "He crazy! He going to steal the election!" Abdul has much to fear if the president were to steal or even win the election. The Muslim ban could morph into a Muslim purge, the president's SS goons going door-to-door. And who would stop it?

—Researchers estimate the president's campaign rallies have likely resulted in thirty thousand positive cases of the virus and at least seven hundred deaths. Two days before Election Day, he is flying to four or five rallies a day in battleground states, killing his own voters in a kind of gruesome cabaret. He accuses doctors of lying about the number of cases in order to get more money from the government.

—Eleven days before the election.

—More than eight hundred people in the U.S. dying every single day.

—The Heat and the Lakers battle in the NBA Finals. Before each game, the players link arms and kneel, VOTE stitched across the chests of their warm-up jerseys. Richard is rooting for the underdog. A Miami upset. He wants the games to continue as long as possible, with marathon overtimes.

—In an interview, the president spews a river of gibberish to describe his experience with the virus: "I felt pretty lousy . . . But I'm back because I'm a perfect physical specimen and I'm extremely young . . . Now what happens is you get better. That's what happens, you get better . . . I'm a senior. I know you don't know that. Nobody knows that. Maybe you don't have to tell them. But I'm a senior . . . I want you to get the same care that I got. You're going to get the same medicine. You're going to get it free, no charge, and you're going to get it very soon."

—George Floyd Square becomes the official name for the section of Chicago Avenue in Minneapolis from East 37th Street to East 39th Street where Floyd was murdered.

—Dead bodies. Richard wants to see dead bodies. Gaping mouths after the tubes are removed, human shapes wrapped in sheets from head to toe, the white-wrapped cargo drawered in hospital morgues and stacked in refrigerator trucks. He wants to see the tear-wracked faces of wives and lovers and sisters and children. If enough Americans see the truly dead rather than the statistical dead, this will be conclusive evidence of the president's reign of mass murder.

—The results of Lina's autopsy: a fentanyl overdose, from the last syringe she ever used.

The advancing days and weeks acquired a troubling urgency, as if the debacles facing the country—pandemic, racial reckoning, economic collapse, an electoral coup—were building to a firestorm.

Three fronts were expected to blow in off the Bering Sea that weekend. While the skies were still clear, Richard and Beth invited their friends over for outdoor drinks. David and Dolores, who had just become grandparents, and Mitchell and Eve, in town while remodeling continued on their second home near Phoenix. The six of them had been gathering together for nearly twenty years. Long dinner parties. Many bottles of wine. Easy and frequent laughter. Eve always brought them gifts. This time, she arrived bearing two designer face masks.

Richard lit the piñon fire and arranged their outdoor electric heater to create a homey aureole of warmth. The string of party lights encircling their backyard winked in the dusk, the leaves of the clematis and bamboo silently fluttering. They sat with separate side tables, each with plates of olives, carrots, cheese and pancetta. Planes descended overhead. Two years ago, Richard had dubbed this The Flight Path Lounge.

Beth made Senegalese chicken soup and ladled it into mugs, the broth rich with peanut butter and spices. They drank a Cabernet and a Pinot Gris. Dolores brought up the previous night's vice-presidential debate. It took place in Utah with plexiglass shields separating the two candidates. The only things that made an impression were the crash test dummy's unctuous pantomime of civility and the house fly that landed on his placemat of short, white hair.

"Black flies matter," Eve said.

Richard had watched the fly on his head for two full minutes and wished the vice president and the fly were in Brundle's teleporter and that someone would flip the switch.

Mitchell refilled their glasses and they all began to talk with guarded hope about how the president was headed to certain defeat. Richard reiterated his fear about voter suppression. Beth brought up the promising reports of early Democratic voter turnout in Wisconsin. Dolores mentioned the possibility that the president would attempt to mobilize underground militias to keep him in power. It was only that morning that thirteen men were arrested for engineering a plot to kidnap the governor of Michigan and take over the statehouse. They called themselves the Wolverine Watchmen, a name that sounded like a Saturday morning cartoon or a teenager's graphic novel. Their mug shots appeared on a Detroit news website. The men's faces were a Neanderthalic ruin of matted facial hair, splotchy red skin, foreheads like plinths.

Beth wished the president would relapse.

"Wouldn't that be great?" David said.

"He's going to be just fine, unfortunately," said Mitchell.

"People are pissed off," said Dolores, "and people who lost people are pissed off. He's minimizing the virus that killed their loved ones."

"And I don't think they're going to forget," Beth said, hopefully.

"I'm not so sure," Richard said. "I think the president could rape a child on live TV and then murder that child with a chainsaw and he wouldn't lose a single voter."

"They'd probably cheer him on," said David.

"Who woulda thunk that a pandemic would have made things even uglier in this country," said Eve.

"Yeah," said Richard. "If a deadly contagion can't bring the country together, nothing will."

"What about aliens?" David asked.

"You mean like . . . ?"

"An alien invasion, yes."

"A *War of the Worlds* type thing?" Mitchell said.

"Nope, wouldn't work," said Eve. "The red-state tribe would want to exterminate them."

"And the blue-state tribe would assign them an acronym," said Richard.

They laughed. A brief silence. It was cozy inside the cocoon of heat generated by the lamp and the fireplace. Mitchell refilled their glasses.

David said, "In about two weeks I'm going to help my son harvest his marijuana plants. That will hopefully get me through the next few months."

Eve chimed in. "I once believed I'd never be friends with anyone who hadn't taken LSD."

Richard and Beth confessed they'd never tried acid, but they had snorted cocaine in their twenties, and had sipped mushroom tea in Koh Samui while on their honeymoon, eating the soggy chunks of psychedelic fungi at the bottom of their glasses, and then enduring a hellish few hours of paranoia in their five-dollar-a-night seaside bungalow.

"If I could get my hands on some LSD, you bet I'd take it," said Eve with conviction.

Mitchell refilled their glasses and commented on the music playing in the background. Hawaiian. The soundtrack to *The Descendants*.

"Can you make us some CDs for the road?" he asked Richard.

"When do you leave?"

"Tuesday." They were driving back to Arizona. They invited everyone down to visit them next February or March. No one could predict what life would look like then.

The fire began to fade. They drained their wine, put on their masks, and carried the glasses and the soup mugs and spoons into the kitchen. They said goodbye. There was a sense that this might be the last time they would be together for several months.

. . .

Masked schoolboys in Nairobi.

An elderly woman breathing through an oxygen tube in a hospital in Kabul.

A woman sitting alone in a chalked circle in Ourém, Portugal.

A testing site in Qingdao, China.

The remaining postcards were stamped and sent to voters in South Carolina. Beth dropped their own ballots in a box near their community center. They considered giving more money to certain candidates in close races but the campaigns, all of them, were engorged with cash. There was so much money that you had to wonder why food stamps and homelessness and Go Fund Me campaigns for sick children should even exist in a country this obscenely rich.

A masked little boy peeking out from behind a 1952 Chevy in Havana.

A nurse weighing a newborn in an apartment in Caracas, surrounded by the baby's unmasked siblings.

Delivering supplies via a basket and pulley to high-rise families in Myanmar.

Voters masked and distanced in Atlanta.

Their Crosstrek was scheduled for a tune-up, even though they'd only put three thousand miles on the car in the last year. He drove to the dealership in Renton, a working-class suburb in the long metropolitan sprawl south of Seattle. Richard remained impressed by how many businesses had adapted to this new world of mask requirements, social distancing, tightly scheduled time slots, and ubiquitous bottles of hand sanitizer. The ceaseless gyre of profit and loss continued with efficiency, all transactions now negotiated by swipes and taps. Greenbacks were nearly obsolete, like the runes of a lost civilization. Richard left the car at the service center, with two hours to kill.

His walk took him past business parks, the buildings with darkened windows and *For Lease* signs. He walked down a dead-end road to a footpath that ran parallel to the railroad tracks on one side and the forgotten Black River on the other. The path had been turned into a walking-and-biking lane with blacktop and split-rail fencing and posted historical plaques telling the story of the Lushootseed, a name describing both a language and the collection of Salish tribes that thrived in Puget Sound, like the one that lived and fished along the Black River. Radiocarbon dating determined that hunter-gatherers lived here as far back as the sixth century. They wore straw hats that looked like overturned baskets. Fished for salmon, cod, and halibut. Harvested clams and collected camas. The river was the drainage for the south end of Lake Washington until it was blocked off and left to dry, the Lushootseed picking up the last of the fish gasping for air along the mucked bottoms. Now nothing remained but a channel of static brown water, banked against a riparian wetland, an oasis for ducks and herons, buffeted on all sides by several square miles of now-vacant buildings.

He zipped up his rain jacket and pulled the hood over his hat. The brisk, wet air was invigorating, the October forest a living watercolor, with auburn streaks in the second growth, the treetops like struck matches, their leaves floating to the ground like ash. The moist sponge of fallen leaves, the fluted tree bark, the bristled grass, the fertile smell of damp earth, and a far-off scent of woodsmoke. The trail connected with another paved path that followed the contours of the Duwamish, a dogged plow of a river whose clean headwaters sprouted from the foothills on the western flank of Mt. Rainier and then slagged through the industrial flats of Seattle before leaking into Puget Sound.

He walked under a railroad trestle and past a sweep of mown lawns and soccer pitches and picnic tables, sectioned-off fields, a stadium, a playground, a pond, a building the size of an airplane hangar housing a restaurant, an espresso bar, a brewpub, indoor squash courts, and a gym. All were closed.

He peed behind a tree, looked out on the deserted playfields, and wondered how long before the sports park withered in its abandonment, reduced to the cliched visuals of end-times Hollywood: Weeds pushing up through concrete. Torn nets. Rusted chain-link fencing. Trash blowing through the grandstands. Squatters burning park benches for warmth.

Despite the reviving air, the five miles of exercise and solitude, the oil change and the nail pulled from a rear tire—a slow leak that had vexed him all summer—he drove home in an unsettled state. Several fronts in the war against the virus were converging all at once. He needed to be on guard against battle fatigue and carelessness. He needed to keep his spirits up amid the waning daylight, the darkness that now fell in the late afternoon. He needed to find the optimism in the everyday. He needed to live like his life depended on it.

With Halloween coming up, he revisited a film he'd first seen twenty-five years earlier, *Habit,* a vampire movie shot on Super 16 mm and directed by an under-the-radar indie veteran, Larry Fessenden. The film was made in cramped New York walk-ups, guerilla-style, without permits, stolen scenes from outside grocery stores, party sequences with friends, grainy exteriors and dim interiors. These kinds of conditions rarely produced meaningful or lasting impressions, but he wanted to see if it said anything about the time they were living in now. An alcoholic waiter meets a mysterious girl. They have ferocious sex. She bites him repeatedly and laps up his blood. He gets sicker and sicker. He wonders if he is contagious. The life drains out of him. *Habit* is a portrait of bleak anonymity, lonely death, sickness as an addiction. While watching, happily alone in his studio, Richard could see the weakened shards of late October sun stabbing through the blinds.

Movies continued to save him, as they always had, from real-world desperations. They were his refuge, ever since he was seven years old. Movies were his friends and his teachers, helping him to make sense of a busted childhood, his brother's death, his parents' sad and angry divorce, his place in the new order of things. He learned about love and loyalty, about violence and betrayal, about hate and sex. He learned how to be alone with himself, to not fear solitude. Beth respected this, his need to sink into the fictions of the movies in order to make sense of the fret that hovered just beyond the frame in real life. As he tabulated the hours spent watching, keeping a list of titles, directors, and a rating for each movie, he could one day look back at the films that marked the passage of the pandemic, that marked *him*.

Halloween morning.

A few neighbors had constructed elaborate chutes made out of PVC pipe to slide Snickers bars to the trick-or-treaters. Others planned to toss Skittles from second-floor balconies. Many kept their houses dark. Beth's idea was to separate small packets of candy into Ziploc bags and place the bags on a small table six feet from their front porch. Richard lit candles and set them into the emptied belly of a pumpkin that one of Zach's childhood friends had carved for them, the face a terrifying rictus. He arranged the glowing pumpkin near a portable speaker and cued up a playlist of portentous drones and ominous chants, intending to evoke a sense of medieval horror. They plugged in their electric heat lamp and positioned two chairs by their front door, sipping a Zinfandel as the kids arrived on their stoop in a parade of costumes. Furry dinosaurs. A fairy. Something to do with a rabbit's ears and a cape. Beth said hi to the new parents in the neighborhood. They commented on the pumpkin. "A young friend carved it," Richard said. "We aren't allowed to handle knives."

In some ways, Halloween during a pandemic was more relaxing than the usual routine. None of the repetitive answering of the door. The up and down. The open and close. They sat and chatted and replenished the bags of candy. In ninety minutes, it was all gone.

The clocks fell back, and an augury of darkness arrived.

On the day before the election, governors ordered the National Guard to stand by. Business owners nailed sheets of plywood over their windows and doors. Poll watchers from both parties descended on voting sites. The president bragged about his vast team of lawyers, ready to stop the counting of ballots.

Voters in the pink predawn light of a West Palm Beach polling station.

Voters in a Guadalupe, New Mexico parking lot, a string of party lights above them against the pale dawn.

Voters in Michigan, wearing puffy coats and hoodies and ski caps and masks, stretched along an icy sidewalk, waiting their turn at a polling station.

A video showed king-cab pickups flying flags for the president as they circled around voting sites, honking their horns and running stoplights. The red-hatted men and leather-skinned women were tattooed, outfitted in camo and cosplay. They carried guns. Some wore knives strapped to their thighs that were large enough to disembowel a bear.

Beth had stashed a bottle of champagne in the back of the fridge on election night. They expected a celebration, victory for the Democrats across the board: The Senate and the House and the presidency. But as the returns from Florida started coming in, hundreds of thousands of votes were being cast for the president. MSNBC anchors and NPR reporters began a process of emotional compartmentalization, reminding voters that Florida was never a lock for the challenger and that he had many other pathways to election. They were telling viewers to prepare themselves for the possibility of, if not a Democratic defeat, then something much less than the landslide victory they had hoped for. There would be no shellacking or thumping of the president.

Munching on a few nuts, trying to gin up some inkling of a festive atmosphere, Richard imagined for a moment what life would be like under four more years of the president's reign. He recalled a trip he and a sportscaster made to Moscow in the mid-eighties during Glasnost, shooting a series of news features about the Goodwill Games, an attempt by a Seattle businessman to promote friendship between the U.S. and Russia through competitive sports, a kind of cable-access version of the Olympics. One day, they visited the apartments of a group of painters and writers and poets, artists who had been living in a collective for decades. The artists shared their paintings and poems and described their survival strategy for living through revolving regimes of Soviet dictators. They said the key was to ignore politics, to tune out the bellicose edicts and threats and state-sponsored wars. They shared their work with each other and their small audiences, they drank vodka and listened to music, they danced and laughed and played with their children. In other words, they pretended that politics had nothing to do with their lives. They created a world of words and color and love and friends that no authoritarian could take away. The artists said they had no other choice, really, since protests led to lengthy prison terms, which would separate them from their families and their art, their only reasons for living.

Richard wondered if he and Beth would confront a similar reality one day. They had already talked of cutting themselves off from the minute-by-minute addiction of news alerts, the circular grind of punditry and think pieces and agenda-driven nonfiction. He was trying to convince himself that life in a dictatorship was survivable, as long as they had the proper mindset. He feared for his children, but they were perhaps more prepared than he was to live under an authoritarian thumb. Zach had recently been interviewed about his film for an online newspaper. The movie was now in postproduction, only weeks away from completion. He was asked if he thought the pandemic was changing the way people value art.

"I hope it reinforces the idea of how essential art is," he said. "I would describe art as intrinsic rather than just important. I don't really think that we can live without it."

By ten o'clock, it was clear there would be no declared winner that night. There was still a vast gulf between the challenger and the president in Wisconsin, Michigan, and Pennsylvania, but votes continued to land in the Democrat's column. He delivered a short statement to the country stating his team was very confident of victory. The president also spoke, claiming massive fraud, calling for all vote counting to stop immediately.

At two-thirty in the morning, Richard woke up. He blinked at the ceiling, then eased himself out of bed and tiptoed downstairs. Zoomie padded down from upstairs and stood by the front door, asking with a soft meow to be let outside. Richard lay on the couch and closed his eyes, hoping to fall back to sleep. An hour later, he checked the latest numbers in Wisconsin.

In the last four hours the gap in the state had shrunk. Richard blinked and rubbed his eyes and checked his phone again, not believing what he saw. Even though a few thousand votes remained to be counted, analysts predicted the Democrat was close to securing victory there. In Michigan, the same story. A large early lead for the president had shriveled. In Pennsylvania, the president's six-hundred-thousand-vote lead showed the same trend: A few million votes remained to be counted, and the vast majority were expected to go to the challenger.

Richard's bleak mood lifted like a set of blinds. He could hear Beth rustling in their bedroom above him. He stood up and went into the kitchen to make the coffee. Zoomie looked at him through the backdoor window.

"Hey, Zoom," he said as he opened the door, "America might not be fucked after all."

While the water boiled, he checked the vote tallies from other states. The challenger had the lead in Arizona and was close in Georgia, where the *Times* and the *Post* had him as the favorite, but it would likely be days before he could be declared the winner, and the margin of victory would be thin. Somehow, against all normal concepts of sanity and shame, the incumbent had himself collected more than seventy million votes.

"How is that even possible?" Richard said aloud to himself. For months, he had been ticking through a mental checklist of the president's atrocities while in office and assumed he would lose millions of voters, that they would tally his lies and blunders and cruelties and they would flee like escapees from a grisly house of horror. But, apparently—*astonishingly*—not only had these voters clung to the president during his descent to the bottom, they had also dropped with him through that trapdoor. They liked what they saw. They liked swimming in the president's sewage of grievance and insult.

Richard turned on CNN. The monitor screens displayed maps of the country, the allotted electoral votes in each state, and the number of votes won so far by the two candidates. The anchor kept tapping on the screens. He enlarged sections of the map and then minimized them, sending them back to their digital cubbyholes. He tapped. He zoomed. He held notecards and a phone in his hand, using the phone's calculator to tabulate percentages. He updated the information with slight differences in tone each time, with subtle shifts in inflection and emphasis. He explained. He updated. He tabulated. He dissected. He tapped. He zoomed. The anchor had the body of a linebacker and the steady calm of a man steering a frigate. He was dressed in a dark blue suit. He could have been wearing a captain's hat and braided yellow epaulets, navigating his viewers through the ice floes of democracy to the balmy port of victory.

Tap. Zoom.

The president and his team of lawyers filed lawsuits in all of the battleground states, claiming mishandled counts and lost ballots. But they had no evidence to back up these claims. Still, the president, now clearly the loser, tweeted: *I won the election. By a lot.* There was the temptation to laugh at the president and his bumbling enablers, but four years had taught everyone that laughing at the president was a mistake. He had managed to escape every scandal and claim every lie a truth and even if these lawsuits were mere noise, they would help to convince his cult that there was indeed fraud merely because the president had said there was.

Tap. Zoom. Tap.

Saturday morning, four days after election day, Richard texted Beth and his two kids to tell them the Democratic challenger had, just seconds ago, been declared the next president of the United States. Beth came in a few minutes later and sobbed in his arms.

When they woke up the next morning, for the first time in four years Richard's first thought was not of the president's most recent insult, the first image to come to his mind was not of the president's mangled scowl, the first sound was not an echo of the lies the president spewed the day before, or the day before that, or the day before that.

Later, out for a walk, Richard passed by Abdul as he emerged from under the hood of an Astro van.

"He win?" Abdul's face was etched with its usual concern, his mask hanging by one ear. "You think it true?"

"Yes, Abdul. He won. It is official."

"But I worry. That man"—even Abdul couldn't say his name—"he not accept it. He says election was stolen."

"All the people counting the votes say they're accurate. There was no fraud."

"You think so?" Abdul could only think of state executions, refugee camps, daily rations of gruel, and planks across sewage-filled ditches. "I am not so sure," Abdul said.

On the Monday after election day, a major American drug company, working with two German scientists, announced they had invented a vaccine that proved effective against the coronavirus in 90 percent of cases. The news sent the stock market soaring. There was talk of millions of vaccine doses shipping by mid-December. The elderly and the frontline hospital workers and the immunocompromised would be the first to be inoculated.

The virus also reacted to the news.

Cases and hospitalizations and deaths escalated, as if Covid was determined to do as much damage as possible before the vaccine could be marshalled to stop it. More than one thousand people died on that Monday. Another thousand on Tuesday, and on Wednesday, and on Thursday. It was like two jumbo jets full of passengers falling out of the sky every single day. Bars closed, again. Movie theaters postponed their openings. Travel plans were put on hold. The virus was an open wound, leaching through the borders of the Great Plains and the eastern foothills of the Rocky Mountains. Rural hospitals were inundated with patients. Doctors again, *again,* pleaded for people to wear masks. Nurses were again, *again,* being interviewed via FaceTime from the front seats of their cars. The scenario was a replay of the replay of the scenario from spring, only it was much more calamitous. This was the predicted third wave, and it was a tsunami.

Fallen leaves carpeted the backyard. Richard and Beth raked them into piles and dumped them into their yard-waste bin. He folded the table they kept on the porch, brushed off the spiders and stink bugs hiding out on its underside, and stored it in their utility closet. Beth swept off the porch while he moved the bench and side table under the awning. He kept the outdoor heater there, too, for reading in the cold mornings to come, and arranged the outdoor chairs around the fireplace. Beth stripped the covers off of cushions and gathered up the outdoor pillows. A November wind then blew through the tops of the trees, and hundreds more leaves fell into the space they had just swept, like the feathers of a mythical bird.

Three days later, he stood on their front porch staring at the rain dribbling from an aluminum sky, waiting for his afternoon coffee to seep through the filtered grounds into his mug in the kitchen. Zoomie came up behind him and meowed, looking out at the drenched catmint and the sodden patch of dirt he used as a toilet. They stared at the rain together for a few more seconds, then he returned to the kitchen to get his coffee and Zoomie dragged his aging body back upstairs to join Beth in her office. Richard sat down at his desk to continue turning his journal notes into a book, with his third-person narrator leading the reader through the far-fetched months of the last year, with its invisible parasites and ludicrous plot twists and laughable improbabilities and outsized villains and a cast of risible supporting characters, all now building to its final act. Maybe the apocalypse he'd feared in March was still coming, but in the Old English sense of the word, as a Great Unveiling. Ugliness exposed. Beauty revealed. In the smallest of things.

15

HOLIDAYS

The supply chains had held. The lights had stayed on. The internet still worked.

Garbage was picked up and public lawns were mowed.

There was wine in the closet and cold beer in the fridge.

There were books to read and films to watch.

The fires warmed and the music he liked was only a fingertip away.

The sun rose and set, and the monthly full moon reminded him that the orbits had held steady.

His wife and children were safe. He was safe.

Thanksgiving consisted of roasted carrots and squash, a salad of brussels sprouts and toasted pecans, mashed red potatoes with garlic, gravy from a box, smoked turkey with cranberry relish, and banana bread with chocolate chips. There were just the four of them this year.

They gave thanks, going around the table one by one. Zach said he was thankful he had the skills to know how to spend time alone, to entertain himself, and he was thankful he lived near his family and could depend on them for advice if he needed it. Beth was thankful for her community of college friends, for her books and writing and teaching. Chloe was thankful for her parents and for her boyfriend for being there while she navigated the grief of the last few months, while she tried to sort out how to readjust to a bruised idea of the future. Richard offered thanks for the people of the country who were clearheaded enough to stave off catastrophe. He believed the curtain had dropped on the freak show in the White House, and that a deep and thorough fumigation would soon be underway. But mostly he was thankful for Beth, his wife and partner of thirty-three years, his best friend, his lover. They moved in rhythms imperceptible to outsiders, with habits and moods honed and burnished by their time together, more than three decades navigating decisions and detours and obstacles, and now, during these days and months of uncertainty and paranoia and imminent threat, they'd stayed the course. Beth had not gone numb. They'd kept their sense of humor. They'd managed to create new work, and together found a way to be true to who they were and had always been, in these most tested of times.

Soon they would mark the winter solstice and begin the slow walk toward daylight.

December 21. Richard's mother would have turned ninety today. What would it have been like if she were alive during the pandemic? She had lived for sixty years on the property where he grew up, fifteen of those years all alone in a mobile home parked in the yard, the rooms stuffed with boxes full of Christmas ornaments and knickknacks, miniature farm children and cowboys in chaps made of porcelain, cabins and wagons designed by Thomas Kincaid, the self-styled "painter of light" who made millions off the sentimental dreams of elderly shut-ins. Her last weeks were spent in a hospital after a hip fracture, and then three weeks in a nursing home. With her congestive heart failure, the virus would have killed her in no time.

Beth's mother, too, dead more than a decade now, who disappeared into the suffocating vapor of Alzheimer's, an already cruel enough existence even without the bewildering protocols of lockdowns and distancing and mask-wearing. He felt relief, a *guilt-free* relief, that neither of their mothers had lived to endure the present.

The Kris Kringle Christmas tree lot was set up next to a Grocery Outlet in the Central District. The store's bargain prices lured in millennials working three jobs, single moms living on food stamps, the formerly homeless, and anyone else who had to count their pennies. Most of the items were past their sell-by dates. People nicknamed it Gross Out.

As they roamed the tree lot, Beth engaged in her usual holiday ritual of body-shaming.

"That one? It's too fat."

"That one is too short."

"You call that a tree? Look at the spindly branches."

"That one has an eating disorder."

They found a squat but masculine hunk of grand fir for seventy-five dollars and brought him home to live with them for a month.

A masked Santa Claus waiting for children in Budapest.

A masked mariachi band playing at an El Paso funeral.

A masked abuelita selling flowers on a Mexico City sidewalk.

Masked skateboarders in Venice Beach.

Masked mothers in Baghdad, picking up their children from school.

Three thousand one hundred and forty people died in one day. The most so far. It was more than had died on 9/11.

. . .

Hard Times in Babylon

Beth taught her last class of the year to a group of retirement home residents via Zoom. They were learning the art of journal-keeping. Acts of retrieval. Calling up the memories from their long lives. She told them to forgive themselves for what they couldn't remember, and to bind into words the scenes they'd carried with them forever. There was an urgency to their listening, a gravity to their questions and to their note-taking. They'd been in isolation since the pandemic began and the solitude had brought forth a kind of atavistic need to pay tribute, to honor their own experiences. Beth remarked that they were the best students she'd ever had.

A doctor in Nogales with his sleeve rolled up, ready to receive the vaccine.

A close-up of a needle penetrating an arm in a Chicago hospital.

An elderly woman vaccinated in New Jersey.

Two days before Christmas, Beth carried in the morning paper and saw the thank-you note from Bob the delivery man.

Thanks so much for the nice card and the $50 and the personal message regarding your appreciation to have a paper and it's service from me. Very thoughtful to do this. Meanwhile, do not let the virus spoil your holidays. Dig in and have fun. I expect 2021 to be better—hard to imagine it could be worse.

Happy Holidays,
Bob

They dug in and had fun. A small but cozy Christmas with their kids. A languid morning of present-opening. An evening poker game next to the fireplace and the twinkling tree. Richard had taught his kids the game when they were in grade school, betting nickels and dimes, playing variations of Seven Card Stud with names like Baseball, Chicago, Follow the Queen. He liked the soundtrack of poker: The plastic clatter of the chips, the raking and stacking of the spoils, the cards snapped on felt during the deal, the called bluffs.

Later he wrote: *Like Bob, Richard expects 2021 to be better—hard to imagine it could be worse.*

A food stall encased in plastic in a Guatemala City market.
    A body wrapped in a white sheet in a London hospital.
    Fresh graves in a Manaus cemetery.
    Boxes of vaccine stacked on a Rochester lawn.

16

FIRST PERSON

Moclips is the last stop on the west coast of the Olympic Peninsula, as far north as you can go before reaching the Quinault Indian reservation. Moclips. A Quinault word meaning "a large stream." It also designates the place where girls were sent when they began menstruating. To me, the translations always seemed interchangeable. The tribe had self-quarantined and was off-limits to non-tribal members. They'd erected barriers on the only highway in and out of the reservation.

Our tiny cabin, only two hundred square feet, sat on the edge of the sweeping, often deserted beach. We first rented it five years ago, taking turns using it as a solo creative refuge. I'd written scripts here and edited films. Beth had written sections of her memoir. The cabin's large window faced the Pacific, with the surrounding houses out of view. I liked going in winter. I was calmed by the rains, the sunlight peeking from the husks of clouds, the rhythmic collapse of the waves on the shore. I liked to sit and imagine I was the last man on earth.

We were together for this one night, before Beth would head back to Seattle. I'd just arrived after the three-hour drive that bisected one of the few counties in the western half of the state where most of the population had voted for the loser in the recent election, if they voted at all. The county was dominated by two adjacent towns, Hoquiam and Aberdeen, that looked perpetually sluiced by the backwash of ebbing tides. Sawmills, vape shops, tiny houses that sunk into the earth like mushrooms.

Beth helped unload the car, stashing the chicken thighs, lamb patties, sausages, and tuna steaks in the fridge. I hauled in Duraflames for the wood stove. I planned to stay on for another week to continue writing this book.

We put on our warm coats, walked the beach, and got caught up on the craziness of the last few days: The stirring and unexpected victory of two Democratic senators in Georgia, giving the new president full control of the levers of power. The ceremonial count of the electoral votes in Congress, with several GOP senators objecting. And the rally held just up the street from the Capitol Building, where the loser exhorted his zombie horde to storm the building and stop the steal. I described the violence to Beth as if it were a montage, one set to Leonard Cohen's "The Future," which had played over the end credits of the movie I watched later last night, *Natural Born Killers,* Oliver Stone's berserk rendering of America's obsession with violence down to a garish reality show.

They smashed windows, fired shots, broke down doors. They shot pepper spray at the capitol guards and the cops. They threw flagpoles, metal crutches, water bottles. One woman, festooned in an American flag and souvenir gear from the online MAGA shop, was shot and killed by a police officer as she broke through a window. Another woman was trampled to death. A cop died after being struck by a thrown fire extinguisher. Two others died of medical emergencies. The senators and representatives were hustled off to offices and conference rooms where they huddled behind locked doors. The insurrectionists roamed through the lobbies and stairways and offices. They wandered without purpose or design or manifesto. They milled about, fingering busts of dead men, rifling through desks like delinquents looking for jewelry. They stuffed scraps of paper into the pockets of their jackets. One guy carried off a lectern, smiling for the camera. Another guy wore a deerskin cape and some kind of headdress with horns. There was a photo of him roaring like a stag. Others wore Kevlar vests and tinted goggles and black helmets. Some carried zip ties that hung from their belts. One man walked through a dark-paneled lobby carrying a Confederate flag the size of a bedsheet. Another put his feet up on a desk in the office of the Speaker of the House and wrote her a note calling her a bitch.

The loser had told his brainwashed tribe that he would march with them to the steps of the Capitol. But instead he retreated to the White House so he could watch the chaos on TV. Four hours later the building was reclaimed by the police. They escorted the insurrectionists out as though they were tourists who got separated from the rest of the group. They chased trespassers off bleachers that had been erected for the upcoming inauguration and told them to go home. They slowly cordoned off the surrounding walkways and streets, shooing the people away, as if it were closing time at a museum. The insurrectionists strolled back to their hotels, excited and victorious.

I had trouble understanding why they were not being detained and arrested. Where are the armed police, the National Guard, the tanks and helicopters and Homeland Security agents? Where is the shock-and-awe juggernaut of the country's militarized law enforcement, the same show of body-armored force that had rained down on Black Lives Matter protestors during the harrowing days of May and June? In the evening, after calm had returned to the capital, the members of Congress reassembled to continue certifying the election.

This morning, the car loaded for my drive to Moclips, I remembered to check our mail before leaving. Abdul was in the alley, removing grease-caked parts from the bed of his pickup.

"Oh ho!" he said. "Did you see?"

There were crinkled lines of a smile around his eyes.

"I know! Amazing!" I said, although I wasn't sure if what I'd watched on TV was a serious attempt at a coup d'état or a pathetic farce.

Abdul chuckled, as though the dervish of events had reached such a swirl that Allah had finally given him permission to laugh about it.

As more reports came in, as videos were posted by the insurrectionists, videos that showed uncontained violence, rabid and angry faces, over-

matched police and security officers, it became increasingly clear how close some of the rioters had come to finding and killing members of Congress. There were rumors of pipe bombs, of militia groups made up of former soldiers and current police officers, of death squads, and even insiders—members of Congress—working with the mob. Someone had erected gallows, where they proclaimed they would hang the outgoing vice president for his part in confirming the results of the election.

Beth and I reached the river that flowed into the beach, dividing Moclips from the reservation. The river swelled and drained with the tides, sometimes with a fierce energy, tearing against the tribal beach to the north and the tourist beach to the south. We followed the river inland, where minerals embedded in the soil turned the water the color of rust, where the river twisted around exposed tree roots and overflowed its banks and seeped into basements when there was a storm at sea. A lone aluminum boat, always in the same place, was tied to a stump, waiting for an owner who never seemed to arrive. We looped through the forest near the river and wandered among ancestral cedars. Microclimates of old growth and bog. Sun, mist, rain, and steam. We lifted our eyes to the grandfatherly spruces. Pushed our hands into bulging sponges of moss. Walked along a narrow gorge frothing with the swell of immense rains. We stepped carefully on slick boardwalks built over a swamp.

    Sword ferns clashed in the sunlight.

    Drapes of moss hung from trees.

    Water seeped up from the earth.

    We heard a liquid breathing.

Later, I wrote:
    So much life.
    All around us.
    So much life.

AFTERWORD

November, 2072

Dear Readers,

As you know, the recent breach of the walls in the Sierra sector has triggered an Emergency Alert for all protected zones in the country. While authorities have arrested and executed the trespassers, all identified as members of the Texas Taliban, there are reports that the virus may have infected several families living along the southern boundary. They are in quarantine, but specialists with Virus Enforcement have detected yet another new and virulent Covid strain within the infected population, and most of them are expected to perish within two weeks. The Total Lockdown order now in place for all protected zones means we are in First Survival mode for at least the next six months. I will continue to publish Where We Stand, but future installments may be sporadic. Thank you for reading.

Patricia Eden

ACKNOWLEDGMENTS

This book probably would have been deleted from my laptop long ago if fellow writer Tom Corvin had not read an early and very lengthy draft, and not pronounced it worthy. This version is much shorter and, I hope, much better. Thank you, my friend.

There were others who read or heard me read pages from the book and offered suggestions and/or encouragement: David, Mike, Caroline, Jesse, Carmen, Lee, Annie, Doug, Dodi, Michael, Ellen. Thank you.

I began writing this book in March of 2020. I churned through several titles and perspectives and word counts in the journey from first page to final edit. I could not have sustained the course without the patience, keen eye, and love of my wife and creative partner, Ann Hedreen, a writer herself, and a teacher of memoir. She also allowed me to use the excerpts quoted directly from her journal entries. Thank you to my daughter Claire Thompson, also a writer and teacher, who copyedited and proofread the final version. Along with my son Nick Thompson, a filmmaker and writer and a tough critic, they both gave me the love and support I needed to see this through.

I was told by consultants that no one wanted to read about the pandemic. If you finished this book, thank you. Please pass it on.

ABOUT THE AUTHOR

Rustin Thompson is a writer, filmmaker, and deejay. He is the author of Get Close: Lean Team Documentary Filmmaking (Oxford University Press) and the director-cinematographer-editor of several feature length documentaries. He hosts two music programs on the independent radio station KBCS.FM, based in the Pacific Northwest. He lives in Seattle with his wife, Ann Hedreen.

Made in United States
Troutdale, OR
02/18/2025